The Other Side of Love

by

MysTory

PublishAmerica
Baltimore

ISBN: 1-4241-7132-6
PUBLISHED BY PUBLISHAMERICA, LLLP
www.publishamerica.com
Baltimore

Printed in the United States of America

Dedication

This book is dedicated to me! I did all the hard work and all! Just Kidding, I want to dedicate this book to all of my friends…and you know who you are! People who know me, know that I don't use that word lightly, so this book is for all (4 or 5) of you!

Acknowledgments

I want to thank everyone who supported and believed in me since day one! I love you all, especially my family and close friends.

Thank you for understanding when I did not immediately call you back and when I was so tired all I wanted to do was sleep! I am on a mission, that will pay out for us all one day!

P.S. Now all y'all advocate readers can STOP calling me about when the book will come out! It's out...now read it already!

Prelude

Ever since I came back into town I've been thinking about Lisa. Naw, for real, I never stopped. My cousin told me she worked at the local department store. I've wanted to go over there just to get a glance, but I haven't built up enough nerve. Plus, if I saw her right now, I would want to jump her damn bones! I haven't seen her in so long. What if she's big? I heard that most people gain weight their first year of college. Shit, I don't care. That's my girl. She'll always be my girl. Yeah, I remember when she used to sneak me to her house. We were in high school, neither one of us knew what we were doing the first couple of times, but it was fun learning. Damn she felt good. I don't even care about her being my first. I was her first too, so who cares. Most niggas lie about their first time, but not me. I can still feel her smooth chocolate skin. Her breast…thinking about her breast I can't help but smile to myself. Most chicks hated on her. She was always bigger than most of them. Damn I miss those guns. The military teaches us to use weapons, but little do they know I was already trained in handling WMSs before I even came to see Uncle Sam. Weapons of Mass Seduction. Damn, those were the days. But that was years ago, before the baby and wife made me become a family man. And many moons before I began to run myself ragged trying to show people I love them regardless of the circumstances.

Chapter 1

The buzzing of the alarm clock roar in my ear as I tried to get up for work. I looked at the clock but continue to let it scream.

"Anthony. Are you awake?" I vaguely heard the question from my wife's mouth.

"Anthony. Did you hear me?" she asked again.

"Yeah, yeah. I hear you. I'm up. Damn."

I slowly respond as annoyed as ever. I don't know which one is worst. Her yelling in my ear or the alarm clock screaming in the other.

"Well, you don't have to catch an attitude. I'm trying to help you out. So you won't be late for work." She easily matched my annoyed tone.

I don't answer her. Instead I get up and walk to the bathroom. I turn the shower on and wait for the steam to invite me in for a wake-up call. I brush my teeth and slowly step into the shower afterward. The water pounces on my body instantly awakening me. I lather and mentally prepare for my day. I hear Maria in the bathroom. I don't say a word. Neither does she. She must have to use the bathroom pretty bad. It's rare that she comes into the bathroom while I'm in the shower. Anymore. When we both were in the military she used to come to my apartment and we'd sleep and shower together all the time. But since Jamaal came, we don't do much of that. Mainly because lately, I've been regretting the marriage part of our deal. I say deal because all I wanted was a baby. I didn't think I'd have to get married too. She was down. I told her how I wanted a baby and how my first and only love, Lisa, would not do it. Maria said yes real quick. I guess I should have taken that as a big ass red flag. But I got what I wanted and at that time, that's all I cared about. About months into the pregnancy Marla came to me with some wedding bullshit. I have to admit it, she got my ass bad. She told me how much money we can get from the military, which wasn't a lie, then she threw in, "Plus, both our families would accept the situation better." My dumb ass agreed, and the next thing day we went down at the justice of peace and said, "I do." I shook my head of the memory and continue to show. Thinking about all that old stuff made me forget all about her being in the bathroom. Suddenly, Maria rips the shower curtain open.

"You called that bitch, didn't you?" she screamed.

"What the hell are you talking about?" I asked, trying to catch my breath from being scared half to damn death.

"You talked to her. I know it. I had a dream about it. Plus, you didn't even say good morning, kiss my black ass or shit, to me this morning."

I am looking at her like the crazy chick she is. Water is spraying all over the floor. From the corner of my eye I see speckles of water hit her in the face, so much that she blinks a lot. I continue to shower, as if the curtain is not open. I try very hard to keep my laugh under control.

"You want to join me? I mean damn, you standing out there will not cleanse you as well as actually getting in the shower," I said.

"Ha. You funny. You make me sick. I am serious. Why are you ignoring me?" Maria tried to sound sincere.

I pull her into the shower, kicking and screaming.

"What the hell is wrong with you? You're getting my hair wet. This is some bullsh—"

Before she could complete her sentence I kiss her. I slowly pull off her clothes and dropped them on the back of the bath tub. I bend her over and slip my man hood into her. She moans. I continue to work her walls as she pants under the trickling waterfall flowing from the shower head. Maria's moans continue to fill the bathroom. The sound echoing from the walls turns me on. I increased my speed and deepen my strokes.

"Come on, baby. Tell me," she pleaded.

I obey. We both explode. I slowly pull out and stand her up. I turn her around to face me. I look into her eyes and kiss her.

"Maria, I love you. I love Jamaal. That's all that matters," I said as I quickly washed in the cold water.

"I know but—"

I interrupted. She moved aside to give me room.

"That's all that matters," I repeated.

I wash the soap off and get out the shower. I dry off, leaving Maria standing in the shower in a daze. Not sure if the daze was from the morning quickie or my avoidance of the whole situation, I walked back into the bedroom to dress. Five minutes later, I heard the shower shut off. By the time she entered the room I was dressed and walking out for work.

"Will you be home late?" she asked before I vanished.

Trick question. "It depends," I quickly answered before she caught me thinking too long.

"I'll call and let you know," I added.

"Okay," she responded as she crawled back into the bed nude.

I walked into Jamaal's room. He was fast asleep as usual. I leaned over and kissed my pride and joy.

"That's my boy," I whispered, heading out the door.

As soon as I got into the car, my cell phone rang. Wondering who the hell was calling me at eight in the morning, I answered the phone.

11

"Speak," I said.

"Sup, man, what the hell you doing?" my cousin, David, asked.

"Nigga, you act like it's three in the afternoon. What the hell you want so early in the morning," I snapped.

"Man, guess who I just saw?" he asked, sounding like an anxious two-year-old playing peek-a-boo.

"Who?" I asked.

"Lisa," he quickly said and waited for a response.

"Word?" I tried to sound as uninterested as possible.

"Word, nigga. Don't try to act like you ain't worried."

My cousin has always known me. And how I've always felt about Lisa. There was a huge amount of silence as I thought about how she looked.

"Ant? What the hell? Man you got it, still! I'm gone," David yelled.

"Um, alright. One," I said, still thinking.

"Yeah, Peace."

David got off the phone. I could have sworn I heard him laughing at me. Shit. I don't care. I'm not afraid to admit how I feel about Lisa. She and everybody else, including Maria, know I love Lisa. Maybe that's my problem. Maybe I love her too much.

I got to work in no time. I know, because I thought about Lisa the whole way. I park the car and head inside. I walk to my desk and sit down. Still somewhat in a daze.

"Lee, what's wit you this morning?" my co-worker questioned.

"Naw, nothing man. I'm straight," I lied.

"Straight hell. You got a woman-done-fucked-me-over look on your face," he said.

"Why you say that?" I asked.

"'Cause you looking like you just got caught screwing in your bed," he said.

"Naw, but remember when we went to camp? I told you about my first love," I asked.

"Yeah, oh shit. She here, ain't she? You know that's why your girl didn't want you to be stationed here. Don't you?" he said, sitting down.

"Yeah man, I know. But I haven't seen her. My cousin told me he saw her this morning."

I said, throwing my cell phone on the desk.

"Yeah? And?" he questioned.

"Well, I've been thinking about her and peep this." I moved closer to the desk.

"Maria bust in the bathroom while I'm taking a shower and screams on me about some dream she had of me talking to Lisa and shit."

At this point I feel myself getting nervous.

"Damn. Maybe you should have stayed in N.C. man. You gonna be walking on eggshells being here."

"Fuck that, my family is here. I'm gonna stay, plus—"

I stopped in mid sentence. I didn't want to say something I'd regret later.

"Plus what?" my co-worker pleaded.

"Nothing. We need to get ready for drill," I quickly shut the conversation down.

"Lee you're a nut case," he said, walking away.

I had to keep my mouth closed. Too many of my co-workers knew Maria, because of their wives or long term girlfriends. I can't risk shit getting back to her ass. I got too much on my plate as it is. I head to the locker room to prepare for our morning drill. The locker room is full of half naked men joking about who's bigger than who. I smoothly join in to keep my mind off Lisa.

"All y'all might as well step to the side, 'cause Daddy is here little lads," I yelled, putting on my wetsuit.

"Fuck you," Baines yelled from the back.

"No thanks, man. I don't go that way. Plus, your mom's enough," I playfully shouted.

"All of you shut your holes. I'm half of y'all little bitches' daddy. And you got thirty seconds to make it to that damn swamp or that's y'all asses!" the head man yelled from the front door.

We all piled out of the locker room like the place was on fire. I refused to be left behind. It was always known that the last became the first for P.T. and not I. Not today or not time soon.

Chapter 2

Tired as all out, I walked into my apartment. I threw my keys on the table and looked around. The place was very quiet.

"Ri-Ri," I called.

No answer. I walked to the bedroom. The bed was unmade and clothes were on the floor.

"Damn. Home all day and can't even keep the house clean," I grumbled.

I pick up the clothes from the floor and place them in the hamper. I make up the bed and head for the bathroom. I take off my clothes while turning in the shower. I always came home after work to shower. It's bad enough we have to change when we get to work, but I figure too much changing around all men may give somebody the wrong idea. It's only twelve of us specials ops, but I'm the only black on the squad. And just in case one of them dudes on the DL. I rather keep my dick to myself for the most part.

I step into the tub and begin to shower. Once I dry off I begin to wonder where the hell Maria was with my son. I wrap a towel around my waist and pick up the phone. I call her cell phone. She picks up after the second ring.

"Hey." She sounded cheerful.

"Sup, man, where you at?" I questioned.

"Oh, I decided to take a trip up to D.C. to see my parents and dem," she answered.

"Damn, can I get a note or some shit?" I demanded.

"My bad. It was last minute. We'll be back Sunday," she explained.

Silence.

"Okay," I say quickly.

I know Maria. This is some type of test her damn mom done told her to try. I know it. Her mom's like that.

"Okay, baby. I'll talk to you later. I'm doing Mama's hair," she said.

"Kiss my son for me," I told her before I hung up with no goodbye. I laid on the bed, thinking. It was Friday. She was gone and I was here. "What the hell am I gonna do?" I asked myself.

Just as if he had read my mind, David called.

"Sup, nigga," I greeted him on the line.

"Chillin', man. What you doing tonight?" he asked.

"Nothing, Maria and Jamaal in D.C.," I said.

"You should've expected that. She didn't want you to come home because you'd be closer to Lisa but she closer to her peoples. She won't complain for long," David preached.

"I guess. Whatever y'all doing, I'm down," I said, looking at my closet door as to peer through the door to search for an outfit.

"Well, we going to Tony's for some food then to the beach. It's summer and you know mad honies down there," he said.

I could almost see the smile through the phone.

"That's cool. I'll be at your house in an hour," I said, agreeing to the plans.

"Aight. One," David yelled.

"One," I returned the exit greeting.

That damn boy is so loud! I shook my head and pulled out some Jean shorts, a wife beater and a long t-shirt. I took my Tims out of the box but left them at the foot of the bed. As I sat on the bed the phone rung. I didn't recognize the number, but answered it anyway.

"Speak."

"Hey, cutie. You busy tonight?" The low but sweet voice rang on the other end.

"Yeah, I got plans why?" I asked.

"We having a party and was wondering if you'd be attending," she stated.

"Naw, I'm out wit the boys, Boo. Maybe some other time," I said.

"Okay. I'll call again," she said disappointingly.

"I'm sorry, really. Maybe next time."

I hung up the phone and got dressed.

"You really need to stop giving out your number so much," I said to myself.

The only thing that kept me cool was the fact that the women I dealt with were always good at keeping our business to themselves. So even if Maria called a number from my cell, she'd never know a thing. A nigga just cool like that. I finished getting dressed and walked out the house. I got to David's house just in time to see him and the guys walking out of the door.

"Y'all was gonna leave a nigga?" I said.

"Naw, we were coming out to get away from Dave's piece," Justin said.

The guys laughed.

"Damn Dave Rita acting up again?" I smirked.

"Yeah. But you know I don't care." He laughed.

"I told you not to give that gurl a key to your spot," Justin said.

"Man J. shut-up. Your girl got your key now. In fact, I gotta leave all early 'cause I got to go to J's crib to handle some shit," I joked.

"Shet. I can't tell, nigga," Justin said, holding his manhood in his hand.

We all hopped in Justin's Navigator and headed to Tony's.

The line was long as usual. People were dressed for the club. Women half dressed and men overly jeweled down like a music video was being shot.

"Nothing's changed," I said.

"You thought they would?" David asked.

"I guess you right," I added.

"Okay Pimps, get out and do the damn thang. Just don't try to bring no bitches back out. They won't fit on the way to the beach." Justin laughed.

I stepped into the place like a hometown celebrity. I had come here last week, when I first got settled, but I was so drunk that I didn't know if I was coming or going. But not now. I'm sober and ready for whatever comes my way. I see many people from my old neighborhood and even school. I walked up to the bar and order a drink. As I begin sipping my Sexi Black and listening to the fellas talk crazy about women, I feel a tap on my lower back.

"Hey stranger how are you?" the woman asked as I turned around.

"Heeeyy, Kim, what's up with ya?" I asked with a smile.

I'm one step closer to Lisa, I thought to myself.

Kim is Lisa's god sister. Talking to her will surely get the message out that I'm home. If she doesn't know already.

"Chillin'. Did you get a call today?" she questioned.

"Yeah. That was one of yours? I was busy, as you can see, I'm hanging out with the boys," I replied.

"Yeah, that was from one of mine. That's cool. We all need a break every now and then," she said.

"True. Hey, your sis know I'm home?" I asked.

"I don't know. I try not to get into all that. Especially since her and Rodney engaged. Why would I mention you?" she smirked.

She must know that Lisa didn't tell me about that shit. I can't believe she did not tell me. What was she thinking.

"Ump," was all I managed to get out.

"Don't be like that. That's ole school luv, plus ain't too much you can do with a baby and wife now!" she smiled.

Bitches be killing me always sticking together. I mean Kim my girl and all but damn! Did she have to throw me that blow like that? I nodded and turn back to face the fellas. Kim must have gotten the point because she spoke to the boys and walked off.

"What Kim want wit her thick self?" David asked, watching Kim walk across the sports bar.

"Just to say hi and to tell me that Lisa's engaged," I said.

"Oh, that's some bullshit. To RODNEY!?" he asked.

"Yeah, ain't that some shit?" I questioned.

"Nigga, let that shet go. Man that was kiddie shet," Justin interrupted, looking tipsy already.

"Man, I advise you to calm down. Ant real serious when it comes to that gurl!" David said, defending me.

"I'm just saying, that shit is old!" Justin said.

I didn't say a word. I needed time to process the situation. I ordered another drink and listened to David talk about every piece of ass that walked pass us.

"Too wide....Lumpy...Damn! Too small...Bootiful!" he commented.

I shook my head and laughed. By the time we got ready to got to the beach Justin was too drunk to drive. I hoped in the driver's chair.

"Look man, don't fuck my shit up," Justin slurred from the backseat.

"Man, I got this lush," I replied.

We got to the beach in no time. It was packed, as we expected. I found a place to park and we got out to walk.

"Lawd, I don't feel like walking," Justin complained.

"You need to walk that shit off because you not staying at my crib, yo," David joked.

"I'll be straight by the time we get back," Justin assured David.

I got out the truck, took my shirt off and threw it on the seat.

"Here his ass go. Nigga, you ain't buff," David joked.

"Don't be a hata," I joked back.

As we began to walk the strip I got a lot of stares and blown kisses. I don't if it is the tattoos, six to be exact, or the point that I'm a tad bit built.

"Look. You better use all this attention to your advantage. Ain't Maria gone?" Justin asked.

All the female attention must be making him sober up.

"I'm cool," I said.

"Well, throw some this way. I'm cool, too, but I'm also horny as hell. I'll use it," Justin said, looking at a very thick, well-proportioned chocolate honey winking at me.

"Go for it, dude. Ain't nobody stopping you," I said.

It was getting late and with the swamp drill we had earlier today, I'm ready to hit the bed with a head first dive.

"Yo, man, it's two in the morning. I'm tired," I said.

"Yeah, me too," David agreed.

"Yeah, let's make this u-turn back to the whip before I pass out," Justin whined.

We were blocks form Justin's ride when David grunted, "Oh my God, here we go."

I look up from my phone, which I was text messaging Maria goodnight. There she was, standing in front of the pizza joint with a slice in her hand, her girls behind her and some nigga trying to spit game in front of her.

"Guess we're not going anywhere now," David playfully teased.

"Shet. I'll meet y'all at the whip," Justin said.

As we got up on Lisa, David and I stopped. The girls with her I'd never seen before. But as I stood there, quite speechless, they laughed.

"Damn, Lisa. You might want to speed the process up, the check out line is getting real long!" one chick said.

"Uh huh," the other co-signed.

Lisa looked up at me and smiled. Being that we had not seen each other since I popped up at her school and all, I did not know how to interpret the smile. The pitiful guy trying to holla gave Lisa his number, reminded her to call him and left. But not before grilling me.

"Nigga, you ain't dat damn froggy," David, said sensing the same heat I had. He turned to Lisa's girls, walked to them and began talking to them. That's my man. The distraction technique gets the friends out the business every time.

Lisa continued eating her pizza as if she was waiting on me to make the first move.

"What's up, baby?" I tried to sound as calm as possible.

"Nothing, Anthony. What's up with you?" she responded.

"Chilling. It's good to see you. You still look good. I heard you engaged," I said.

I looked down at her finger.

"Nice ring," I said.

"Thanks. Yeah," she responded.

"When's the big day?" I asked.

"Dunno. Haven't set one yet." She shrugged.

Good. I thought to myself. I got time. For what, I don't know. I just know I got some.

"I'm not gonna bother you. Just wanted to say something to you," I lied.

I wanted to take her home and bang her out and make her forget all about her, man, but I had to keep playing it cool.

"Oh. Okay. It's nice seeing you." She smiled.

"Can I call you sometime?" I asked.

"I guess," she answered.

She began to take out a pen from her purse.

"Oh, I remember your number. I'd never forget," I said.

"Do you. That's nice but I don't live with my parents anymore. So if you have my number I'd be real surprised," she smirked.

I just stuck my foot in my mouth! Damn.

"Oh, you got your own place. That's good," I said, trying to recover my last statement.

She laughed. I did, too, but for a different reason.

"Yeah, here you go." She handed me a number.

I looked down at it and must have had a puzzled look on my face because she broke my trance.

"It's my cell phone number," she said.

"Good looking." I smiled.

"Now get your crazy cousin before he talks my co workers out their panties. Look at 'em." She laughed.

I looked over at David who had hands all over him from Lisa's co-workers. I laughed again.

"Hey man, c'mon. Justin's waiting," I said.

David broke free from Lisa's girls and walked over to me.

"They some freaks. Damn shame I can't stay." He laughed.

"You dumb." I laughed.

"Bye, David," both girls said in unison.

"Later, babies," he responded.

"Oh, you too, Lis," he teased.

"Bye, boy!" Lisa said, waving him off.

When we left, I heard one of the girls question who I was. I smiled to myself. I would have loved to stay back and hear her response. David was drunk and stumbling by the time we reached J's car. I opened the door, pushed him in and followed.

"'Bout time," Justin complained.

"Nigga, just drive. I'm ready to go home," I said.

"I don't know why, you just gonna spank your monkey. Maria not here," David joked.

"Aight nigga, I ain't going there," I said, looking out the window.

Lisa didn't change at all. She still has beautiful white teeth, a thick shape and sparkles in her eyes. I was never able to resist those sexy almond shaped eyes of hers. Maybe I'll get to see them more often, now that I have her number. We got back to David's house. I didn't even go in.

"Holla," I yelled as I jumped in my car.

All that was on my mind was Lisa. I still felt the stuff I felt when we were in school. I turned the radio on and Avant's "My First Love" blasted through the speakers. "Ain't that some shit," I said out loud. I listened and thought about all the times Lisa used to braid my hair. I chuckled. *Man, you got it bad*, I thought to myself. I got home, threw my keys on the table and jumped in the shower. I never could just come home from going out and then go to bed. Too many germs. Guess that's the military influence. I turned on the shower and got in. I was still thinking about Lisa. I felt my manhood grow long and hard. I tried to ignore it, but couldn't. I reached out for the knobs and suddenly switched the water to cold. I yelled. The water was cold as ice. It worked, though. My boy left just as sudden as he came. I finished my shower and got out. Drying off, I heard my phone ring.

"Who the he—" I said, looking at the clock.

It was four in the morning. The phone was still ringing. I answered.

"Baby? You there?"

It was Maria.

"Yeah, I'm here. What's wrong?" I asked.

"Nothing. I was just thinking about you. What took you so long to answer?" she questioned.

"I was in the shower. I just came in from hanging out wit Dave," I said.

"Oh. I love you," she said.

"I love you, too," I said back.

"Okay. I'm going back to sleep. Bye." She hung up the phone, not giving me time enough to respond. I knew what that was. She was trying to check on me. That was her way to see if I was gonna tell her where I was or if I had somebody there. She thought she was slick. And she won't sleep. She didn't sound asleep at all. She should know better. I would never do dirt in the crib. She has to give me more credit than that. I pull back the cover on the bed and climb in. I close my eyes but only think about Lisa. I turn on the television. A syndicated *Cosby Show* is on. I watch two episodes and close my eyes. My little man is back. I put my hands behind my head to keep from stroking him. I kept my eyes closed as Lisa's voice kept ringing in my ear.

Chapter 3

My panties instantly got wet when Anthony hugged me. He was the last person I expected to see at the beach. I called myself keeping busy while Rodney was at football camp, for the team. It is kind of hard though. Anthony looked damn good too. Damn. He must be stationed here. If he is I don't know if I can deal.

"Lisa, gurl what the hell you thanking about?" my co-worker, Crystal, asked me, punching me in the arm.

"My bad girl. In a daze I guess," I answered while rubbing my arm.

"That shit hurt. Don't hit me no damn more," I said.

"That sexy ass chocolate bar got your nose wide open," Crystal teased.

"Naw, nothing like that. I'm just sleepy," I lied.

I wanted to jump Anthony's bones the minute I smelled that Very Sexy for men on him. I don't know what Victoria was thinking when she made that, but I bet a lot people got secrets because of that scent.

"Yeah, I feel you. I'm ready to bounce, too. Sherry, let's go," Crystal said, turning towards Sherry.

Sherry is a really nice girl, but I really think she allows Crystal to walk all over her and use her. Sherry pulled her keys out of her purse and walked towards her car. I followed suite with Crystal complaining the whole time.

"I don't now why you wear those little clothes everywhere you go. And wonder why people be all over you," Crystal scolded Sherry.

The ride home was quiet, at least for me. I couldn't seem to shake the replay of Anthony towering over me to give me a hug.

"What the hell is with you?" Crystal asked from the front seat.

"I'm cool," I lied.

In fact, I was quite warm. My body was yearning Anthony and like crazy. I just wanted to get home and take a hot shower to ease my body of all the sexual tension it was going through. Sherry pulled up to my apartment door, and just in time, I was just about to go into another day dream about Anthony.

"Okay, gurlie. I think this is your stop," Sherry said with a smile.

"Yes, it is." I sighed.

"Be cool, Lisa," Crystal said with her head out the window.

"I will," I replied.

I walked in to my apartment and instantly began to start peeling off my clothes. By the tine I reached the bathroom I only had on my thongs and bra. I decided not to wait and to just get into the shower while I was standing in the doorway of the bathroom. I turned on the water and then stepped in the tub. The water felt so good on my skin I almost wanted to melt. I stayed in the shower until I was completely exhausted. As I dried off I heard my cell ringing. I rushed out the bathroom to the phone thinking it would be Rodney since I hadn't heard from him all day. I picked up the phone, but didn't recognize the number so I knew exactly who it was.

"Hey, kinda late don't you think," I answered the phone.

"What's up? How you know it was me?" Anthony questioned.

"Who else could it have been? I don't give my number out like that," I said.

"What you doing?" he asked.

"Drying off," I replied.

"Word? You need help?" He sounded excited.

"I think I got it," I said.

"Oh. Anyway. Can I come and see you? I am dying to see you and catch up," he said.

I sat on the phone, contemplating on his offer. I looked at the clock. It was early in the morning. I knew Rodney wouldn't be coming over this late.

"Sure. I don't care," I answered.

I hurried and gave Anthony directions to the apartment. When I got off the phone I scurried, like a mouse, around the place picking up my clothes that trailed from the front door to the bathroom. I lit a tar baby incense and found a pair of jogging pants and a tank top to throw on. That way I didn't have to put under clothes on. I wasn't gonna change that for him! I don't even know why he still attracted me and why I let him come to the crib. As I thought of the answers to those questions there was knock at the door.

"Damn, whatcha do, fly over here?" I asked.

"You got jokes. Naw I was only in the next city over," he replied.

He walked in and I closed the door behind him. When I turned around he was standing in front of me with his arms stretched and wide.

"Come here gurl!" He said with a huge smile.

I fell into his arms like no time had passed between us. He leaned over and hugged me. Almost covering my whole body. Now I remember. This nigga feel so good what was I thinking? I took a deep sigh.

"You feel good," Anthony said, still hugging me.

His speech broke my trance. I stepped back, looked into his eyes and smiled.

"Thanks," I replied shyly.

I walked over to the couch, grabbed the television remote and plopped down. Anthony slowly walked over.

"So what's been up?" he asked.

"Nothing much," I replied, still looking at the television. I didn't want to look at him. I didn't want him to see the emotions stirring up in my head.

"You still look good. I've been thinking about you a lot since I got stationed here. Probably more than I should have," he confessed.

"Really? Oh, you're stationed here now?" I asked as if I didn't know. But my god sister Kim, had told me the very first day she saw him. Plus, I couldn't forget when I saw him at Tony's.

"Yeah, you didn't know? I figured Kim would have told you," he said, amazed.

"You think people ain't got nothing else better to do but to talk about you?" I joked.

"You ain't dat damn fine," I mumbled.

"Huh?" he asked.

"Nothing. I didn't say nothing," I said, recovering from my smart comment.

"Oh, naw, but I'm saying, I just thought she'd tell you," he said.

I didn't reply.

Dead silence filled the room for a short period of time. I was flipping through the channels. The Cosby Show popped through. I decided to be a smart ass.

"So...how's the family? Wife and kid," I asked. Still staring at the television.

"They alright. My son's two," he said.

"Really. That's good. I can't believe wifey let you out this late at night. Don't she want you around for midnight feedings or something?"

"He's two, not two months. He sleeps through the night and shit."

He seemed a little annoyed.

"Oh well, I don't keep up with that stuff."

"You now the difference, though. You trying to be a smart ass!"

"I think I succeeded. You seem annoyed."

"Naw, I expected it all and then some."

"Oh, you did? Why?"

"Because I know what I did was wrong. I should have waited for you. That was selfish of me to ask you to do something like that."

That made me turn away from the television and face him. "You damn right. Now look at you. A kid. A wife. But you here wit me. What kinda shit is that?"

I began to feel years of pressure release from my body.

"And furthermore, do you even love her? HELL. I can answer that. Hell naw. If you did your ass would be home now!" I said.

There. I got it out. I felt pretty good. Anything else I had was trapped inside for later. I calmed down and focused on Anthony. He was sitting on the couch next to me but I barely felt or heard him breathe. He had a blank stare on his face and then he looked down at my hand and grabbed it.

"You right. About everything. I am sorry. I've never loved anyone like I love you. I've always loved you. Nothing has changed," he pleaded.

"Nothing, uh? Yeah, except you have a wife and kid, and I'm engaged," I reminded him.

He leaned over and kissed me. But that wasn't the surprising thing. The surprising thing was that I liked it. I moved back.

"Lisa. I mean what I say. I love you. In fact, my wife didn't want to move here because I told her that I would never love anyone like I love you," he said.

"Why would you tell her that? Did she slap you? She should have, if she didn't. I would've straight punched your ass like a nigga," I said.

"No. She didn't. She understands. She knew how I felt about you when we were just friends in boot camp," he replied.

"Well you're right. While you were just friends in the same bed, I was at school hoping you were okay," I sarcastically said.

"I'm not going there. I said I was sorry, what more do you want from me? You want me to kiss your feet, too?" he asked.

Before I could answer he grabbed my pedicured foot and began to kiss it. Then suddenly he began to suck each one of my toes. I was so in shock that I was speechless. What the hell was going on. I went from straight dissing this dude to him sucking my toes! It felt so good though. I closed my eyes. Why? That was a green light for Anthony and he knew it. He placed my leg in his lap and grabbed my other foot and gave it the same treatment. He slowly moved his hands to my hips and pulled my pants down and then off. He bent over and began to slowly lick around my thighs. Slowly the moved to my mound, spread my lips apart and kissed my clit. I don't know but I think a moan came out my mouth. What was I doing? I thought to myself. But I couldn't say a word. I just laid there. He orally pleased me so well that it only took about three minutes to cum. He cleaned me up with his lips and tongue. I don't know when, but sometime between those three minutes he had taken off his clothes. I looked at him and first time memories returned. He looked basically the same. Just a lot more muscular and with tattoos every where I could see.

"Let me take you somewhere," he said.

"Where?" I asked like a dummy.

"You'll see. Can I?" he asked.

I slowly nodded.

He stuck his manhood in me so deep I gasped. Well I guess more things changed than I really knew. He saw my body's reaction to his massive body and tried to soothe me.

"I'll be good. I won't hurt you. I promise."

He kept his promise. We both enjoyed one another. I came and suddenly he jumped up. I looked to see what was wrong. The way he jumped up you'd think Rodney walked in the place. Then out of no where he came. All over my couch.

"Nigga are you crazy?!" I shouted.

"My bad. I'm sorry. I'm sorry," he said.

He really didn't sound like it. He sounded as if he was just happy that he busted one.

"Shit," I yelled.

"What?" he asked.

"Nothing," I lied.

But I had just realized that I had sex with this man with no condom.

"Dumb. Dumb. Dumb," I said to myself.

We both got dressed. We talked and he left.

I took another shower and went to bed. The very next day I went straight to my doctor for a check up.

Chapter 4

I got home just in time to catch the phone ringing.

"Hello?"

"Babe. What you doing?" Maria asked.

"Nothing. Chilling," I lied.

"Oh, well Jamaal and I will be home tomorrow," Maria announced.

"Aight. What my boy doing?" I questioned to keep her from questioning me first.

"Nothing, running around getting everything he wants from mom," Maria reported.

"Well, you let him get away with that. He two Ri. You need to start nipping some of that shit in the bud before he becomes a bad ass," I said.

"Like his daddy," Maria mumbled.

"Yeah alright." I brushed the comment off.

"Well Baby, I'm gonna go. I guess I should be there around five or so," she stated.

I knew better. That was her way of trying to get me. She says she'll be home "around" a certain time, but I know she could be home at any time. She trying to trick me up. I pretended to take her bait.

"Okay. I'll see you and my boy around five. Listen. Don't let Mal run all over that place. You know how your parents won't say anything, that means you have to keep him in line, okay?" I said.

"Okay, baby," she agreed.

I hung up the phone yawned and looked around the house.

"Damn," I said to myself. I almost forgot how quiet the house could be. I sat on the couch and aimed the remote at the television. Just as the picture came on a large pizza was inviting me to call Pizza Hut. I glared at the television and reached over the arm of the couch for the phone. I dialed the number. A woman answered sounding more like a sex line operator than the local Pizza Hut.

"Thank you for calling Pizza Hut, home of the stuffed crust pizza. May I take your order?" she crooned.

"Damn, baby, what you selling on top of those pies over there? You sound real sexy," I flirted.

The young woman on the phone giggled.

"Well, sir, would you like to her our specials?"

"Does any of them include you?"

"No, sir, How may I help you?"

"So they don't include you? Or am I the lucky man today?"

"Um, uh that's nice, but I am married."

The woman began to sound uncomfortable. So I tried to break the ice.

"Well, hello married, my name is Mr. Lee and I would like to order a large pizza with pepperoni, extra cheese and ham," I ordered.

"Anything else, sir?" The woman cleared her throat.

"No, the total, please."

"That would be seventeen sixty six," she responded.

"Thank you and how long before I pass out ova here?"

"That would be to you in thirty minutes."

"Thank you so much, young lady. By the way, your husband

is very lucky to have some one as sexy as you, especially if you look anywhere near how you sound."

"Thank you, sir. You have a nice night and enjoy your pizza," the woman stated.

I hung up the phone and headed to the fridge. I took a Corona out, popped the top and went back to the den. I closed my eyes as I began to think about the episode Lisa and I had the night before. I hope she really don't think I'm a jerk. I really need to learn how to control my actions when I cum.

"Damn," was all I could say as I thought about how I came all over her couch. Shit, it's leather, I'm pretty sure she could wipe it right off. It just felt so good I couldn't help it. Just as I was going over how wet she was the door bell rung. I shook off my thoughts and answered the door. To my surprise a beautiful bright kiss of sunshine was standing holding the large pizza bag carrying my pizza.

"Mr. Lee?" the woman asked.

"Yes, that's me. Come in so I can get your money," I said.

"Well, I'm not supposed to," she replied.

"I'm not gonna bite, baby. And who will I tell? I'm cool," I insisted.

The woman came in and stood at the door while I went to the kitchen to get my wallet.

"How much is that again?" I yelled from the kitchen.

"Seventeen sixty six, sir," she responded.

I grabbed twenty five dollars from the wallet and headed back to the door. I took the pie and placed it on the coffee table. I extended my hand with the money towards the woman. She began to reach into her pocket to give me change. Then she looked at her hand and back at me.

"Sir?"

"Yes?" I played dumb.

"The pizza was only seventeen sixty six, you gave me twenty five dollars. Do you need dollars or quarters or something? I can't give out—"

Before she could finish I responded. "No love. Whatever is left is yours. As beautiful as you are you deserve it," I said.

"Thank you, sir," she replied.

"If you really want to be thanked. I can do that. How much time do you have?" I smiled.

She returned the smile.

"Damn. You are beautiful," I stated.

This woman was fine. She was bright, with bright hazel eyes, thick thighs and ass. I almost wanted to take her right then.

"Thank you, sir, but I need to get back to the store."

She hurried out the door towards her car.

"If you are free come back when you get off," I yelled.

I looked around to make sure no nosey neighbors were looking. The pizza woman did not respond, yet quickly pulled off. I watched her car speed off and I closed the door. I grabbed the pizza and carried it to the kitchen. I piled a plate with as much pizza as possible and plopped down in front of the tube. I settled for an episode of Saturday Night Live. As the credits were rolling I became sleepy from eating all that pizza, I vaguely heard a knock at the door.

"Who da he-ll," I stuttered, tripping to the door.

I opened the door and almost fainted. It was the pizza girl. I smiled.

"Was that a bluff?" she asked.

"What?" I questioned.

"Your invitation."

"Naw. I was serious. Just didn't think you would take me up on it," I shockingly responded.

"Well can I come in or should I go home?" she threatened.

I gently grabbed her hand from her hip and guided her inside my home.

"Have a seat," I directed.

"Now what was all that smack you talked on the phone and when I delivered your pizza?" She smiled while getting cozy.

"Oh shet. That was you? So you wanted to see the Don?" I playfully teased.

"Don, uh? Of what? What makes you a Don?" she asked.

"You'll see," I said.

"Where's your restroom? I know I look a mess."

"Down the hall to the right," I replied. As she found the bathroom I stood in disbelief. I could not believe home girl was in my house. I shook my head. I went to the kitchen to grab another Corona. As I turned around to go back to the den, she was standing at the entrance of the kitchen with only a lace matching thong and bra set.

"Damn. Pizza Hut running strippers too!? Why you need to wear sexy draws to Pizza Hut?" I smirked.

"You don't think I'm sexy anymore?" she asked seductively.

"Hell fucking yeah," was all I could get out before she hopped on me, wrapped her legs around my waist and planted a long kiss on my lips. Normally, that shit is a double hell naw for me, but she caught me off guard.

"I see, I have to be on alert with you," I teased.

"Why? You the police?" she teased back.

"Well, let me show you my stick," I said, placing her on the couch, sliding her thong to the side to take car of business.

"Wait!" she shouted.

I paused dead in my tracks and gave her a *what's the matter* look. She reached in between her huge, round melons and pulled out a condom.

"Here, Mr. Alert. You think you'll need this?" she laughed.

"My bad, lady, I'm tripping," I apologized.

"No problem, Pa. Do your thang." She signaled for the go.

I slid the condom on my fully erect penis and entered ole girl like a midnight snack.

We pumped, squeezed and teased each other until we couldn't cum anymore.

"Damn, pa. Had I know, I would have delivered pizza to your ass earlier," she panted.

"Really? Look. you Puerto Rican?" I curiously asked.

"Yes. How'd you know?" she asked.

"The accent and calling me *Pa* gave it away. So do you fuck all your customers?"

"Naw, just the sexy ones!" she laughed.

"No, for real. I usually just answer the phones and take orders, but when you played with me like you did, I had to get a look at you."

"Word?"

"Yeah, word Pa."

"That's something. I never had pizza and pussy delivered by the same woman in the same night," I teased.

"Well, consider yourself served. What time is it?" she asked.

I looked down at my watch. "B-O-Y five."

"Damn. I gotta go," she said, hustling to gather her things and get dressed. I put my boxers on and watched her. She was intriguing, to say the least. Body fine. Teeth white. Hair down to her ass. She was fully dressed and heading to the door by the time I got up.

"It was nice, Mr. Lee," she whispered in my ear as I stood behind her.

"Anthony and you?"

"Stephanie. Nice to meet you. I hope you sleep well." She teased me with her eyes as she left.

I stood in awe, not believing what had just happened. The smell of sex brought me back. I quickly began cleaning up and spraying the house with air freshener. I jumped in the shower and put on some clean boxers. I laid on the bed pulled back the covers and looked at the clock. It read seven a.m. I breathed a huge sigh, not of relief but of tiredness. I was truly exhausted.

It seemed as if I only slept a few minutes before Jamaal came in playing with my eyelids.

"Daddy, you sleep?" he yelled, pulling at my eyes.

"Yes, babe boy. I am."

"Daddy? Daddy DADDIEE!"

"Okay, son, I'm awake. I said, slowly rising to see my son jumping up and down.

By the time I stood up and focused in on the room, I saw Maria standing in the doorway smiling.

"What's up with that?" I asked.

No response.

"Why are you cheesing so much?" I rephrased my question.

"No reason. I am just happy to see you, baby," she finally responded.

Bullshit, I thought to myself. *She ain't never been "happy" to see me. She really need to stop playing with me.* I just smiled and turned to Jamaal still jumping.

"So, lil' man, What's up? What you do at Nanna's?" I asked.

"Nuffin. I eat chickens," he said excitedly.

"Really. Chicken and what?" I asked.

"Applesauce," he replied.

I smiled and turned to Maria. "How was your weekend, Miss?" I questioned my wife, who was now unpacking her overnight bag.

"It was fine. I was glad to have some much needed family time with my parents and sisters. And you?" she asked.

"I didn't do much. Chilled with the boys and ate pizza last night. It's some more in the fridge, if you want it," I said.

"I am tired from the drive, plus Jamaal has been up since four this morning talking about playing and shit," Maria said, taking her clothes off and heading to the bathroom.

I can't even lie. Although Maria gets on my nerves something proper like, she is still sexy to me. I got to give it to her. She does stay somewhat in shape. She is starting to put on a couple of pounds but I see it as more cushion.

"Mommy don't have no shirt on," Jamaal announced.

I looked at the time.

"Damn, noon already," I said to myself.

I picked Jamaal up and carried him to his room.

"You tired, man?" I asked.

"N-O, no, no, no. I not tired," he sang.

"Well, Daddy thinks that it's time for you to take a nap. You've been up for a long time," I said.

"Ah daddy. I don't want to," Jamaal pleaded.

I placed him in his bed and laid beside him until he fell asleep. I got up and walked into the bedroom where Maria had gotten into the bed.

"Ri, that boy was tired. Trying to tell me he won't," I said.

I plopped down on the bed and turned towards her. Her eyes were closed.

"I see he's not the only one," I said. I leaned over to kiss her on her forehead. I got into the bed myself to get some much needed sleep. I turned on my side and blanked out.

Staying still until Anthony was snoring, Maria tried hard as she could to continue to pretend to be asleep. She almost threw up when he kissed her on her forehead.

"This nigga think he slick," Maria said to herself.

She waited a few minutes longer to ensure he was asleep and then got out of the bed. She tipped toed out of the bed room into the kitchen. She looked around and found nothing. She walked over to the phone and checked the caller I.D. She found no numbers different, from the usual, Pizza Hut, Anthony's sister, his parents and his cousins.

"I know he did some dirt this weekend. I just know it," Maria mumbled. Maria walked over to the living room. She turned over the pillows on the couch, looked under the couch, the love seat and even the decorative rug.

"Damn, this nigga was chill this weekend?" she asked herself. She stood in the middle of the floor and thought. She only had one last place…the bathroom in the hallway. She felt Anthony could not possibly be dumb enough to take a chick to the master bathroom, plus, she had already been in there and she saw nothing out of the ordinary draws and socks. She scurried to the guest bathroom and looked around. She tired to smell for a different fragrance from the normal peaches and cream she used in there. She pushed back the shower curtain. Clean and dry. She even dumped out the trash can, but saw nothing in there but paper towels. She sighed and headed back to her bedroom. Maria pulled back the covers, got into the bed and spooned Anthony's body. Anthony's snoring paused as he cuddled into Maria's spoon. Maria felt that this would be the perfect time to make love to her husband. Jamaal was asleep and time was on her side. She slid her hand around Anthony's shorts and to the front of his body. She began to rub his stomach, sliding up to his chest and gently pinching his nipples. She knew this would catch his attention. Anthony backed up into Maria's body leaving no room for movement between their bodies. Maria continued with her "feel-up" session with Anthony. She took her hand and slid it down his boxers and began to caress his semi harden penis.

"Mmm," Anthony moaned.

Maria continued her massage. Anthony had had enough, he turned to face his wife. He placed his arms around her and kissed her seductively. Maria scooted down and kissed Anthony's chest. She continued to travel down until she reached his fully erect penis. She grabbed him with her right hand and wrapped her lips around him. She took her tongue and softly teased the head and then the slit on top. She flicked her tongue from side to side in a wind shield wiper mode. Just as Anthony began to squirm, she shoved his whole penis into her mouth and softly sucked until she slightly gagged. That made Anthony lose it. He began to shake and feel all over Maria's hair.

"I'm about to cum, baby," he informed her.

"Cum on. Cum in my mouth, Daddy," she replied.

Anthony always loved when Maria took it like a trooper. It always felt so good to him when she kept her mouth around him as he came.

"Ah, Ah, oooohhhh." And with that Anthony came as hard as he had ever cum since he and Maria were in boot camp, Maria sucked him dry until he was laying in the bed shivering, as if an arctic breeze had swept through the room.

"Damn, baby, what was that for?" he asked.

"Oh because I missed you, babe," Maria lied.

She couldn't possibly tell him the real reason. That she was giving him apologetic head, because she thought he had another woman in the house.

"Well, I missed you, too. Had I known it was like that I would have come to you in D.C." Anthony laughed.

Maria smiled, hoping he would return the favor but she couldn't count on it. It had been so long, before Jamaal to be exact, since Anthony had licked her right. She had just wished it would be different today.

Anthony turned Maria on her back and hopped on her.

I knew it, she thought to herself. Her wishful thinking of getting a tongue lashing by Anthony was just that. Wishful thinking.

Anthony entered her and began to sex her like she had been gone for years. She couldn't believe it. Although he didn't lick her kitten, like she had hoped, he still had the best dick she had ever had. Maria laid there in ecstasy as Anthony worked her over. She couldn't even count the different positions Anthony had her in. But ending in her favorite got the best of her. Anthony flipped her on her stomach, pushed inside of her and stroked her down. He grabbed her hair and after ten strokes the eleventh made her bust her head on the head board, not to mention cum so hard that the bed was completely wet underneath her. She was exhausted but the sounds of bliss from Maria's mouth woke Jamaal up.

"Ma-mmie," Jamaal shouted.

"I must have woke him up." Maria sounded regretful.

"I told you to close your mouth." Anthony laughed.

"Go get him, Mommy," he teased.

Maria got up, rushed to the bathroom to clean up and throw on clean clothes. By the time she reentered her bedroom, Anthony and Jamaal were lying across the bed watching television.

"Ant. You know the be—"

Before she could finish, Anthony pulled back the covers to show Maria that he had placed a big beach towel in the wet spot she had previously created. Maria smiled. She always felt good when Anthony could read her mind and finish her sentences. She felt a connection with him when he did that. Maria went into the kitchen to begin dinner while Jamaal and Anthony continued their father and son time.

Chapter 5

"Okay Lisa you are a young healthy woman...again," Dr. Levi stated sarcastically.

"Thank so much Dr. Levi."

"Okay, now what is going on Lisa? You've been very paranoid about your body lately. Are you okay?" Dr. Levi concernly asked.

"Naw doc. I'm straight. A new...well um, old friend came home and one thing led to another and I fu—, I mean messed up by having unprotected sex with him," I confessed.

"Well, Lisa, you know how I feel about carelessness. There is no room for it. People are dying from unprotected sex," Dr. Levi said in a motherly tone.

"I understand. It won't happen again," I said.

I felt really bad. I would have felt like shit if Dr. Levi would have told me I had something. Anthony says he loves me, but he's done that before and ended up having a family.

"Lisa. Just be careful okay? I just hate to see someone so sweet with so much potential get caught in a bad situation," Dr. Levi lectured before walking out of the room.

I nodded and prepared to leave. On the way out of the office a girl, that looked very much like she was in high school, walked in with baby in her arms. I was in disbelief. I just could not imagine having a kid at this point in my life. On the drive home I vowed to myself never to place myself in danger like that ever again. I took my cell phone out of the arm rest and noticed I had missed four calls.

Damn, Kim all four times. What does she want now? I thought. I reached down, grabbed my ear piece and called her.

"What up, hooker?" I asked Kim.

"Not a damn thang, gurl," she replied.

"Then why the hell you call me four times!"

"Oh, I don't remember now. But anyway, what you doing?" Kim asked.

"On my way to da crib to get some sleep."

"Where you been?"

"Momma? Is that you?" I teased.

"Bitch, I ain't ya moms. Too beautiful for that."

"Oh, you call momma ugly? I'm gonna tell her, too," I teased.

"Don't do that Ho. She'll kill me."

"And I know," I said, laughing.

"Look, call me when you wake up aight?" Kim demanded.

"Okay, sis."

I hung up the phone just as I reached my drive way. By the time I reached my bed room, I had stripped down to my panties and bra. Perfect for me to just hop into bed. I climbed into the bed and settled down to go to sleep.

Rrinnnnggggg. The phone almost gave me a heart attack. I jumped out of the bed and searched for the phone. It was still ringing. I flipped over in the bed to find the phone under my pillow. I quickly answer.

"Hello?"

"Miss Thang. What's up?" my best friend, Lynelle, screamed in my ear.

"Sleep," I moaned.

"Sleep, why the hell you sleep in the middle of the damn day? What, you pregnant?" she joked.

"Hell naw! I just came from the doctor so I know that ain't what's up," I said.

"Doctor? For what? You okay, chicken? You ain't clapping are you?" Lynelle teased.

"Naw, I'm bout as silent as a graveyard," I returned.

"Well, call me when you get up," Lynelle said.

"I will," I replied.

I hung up the phone. Placed the phone under two pillows this time, placed the covers over my head and attempted to go back to sleep. I began to fall into a deep slumber. And then that's when it begun.

I was standing at the entrance of the church doors, waiting to enter. Lynelle was standing beside me. She had on a beautiful strapless lavender dress, diamond tear drop earrings, a matching necklace and bracelet. Her face was made up beautifully.

"You okay girl?"

"Of course. Why wouldn't I be?" I replied.

I looked down at myself, my Vera Wang shoes were all white and I had on a dress, also white, that fit me perfectly. Lynelle placed a mirror in front of me. I admired my naturally made up face and upsweep.

"Here goes. Let's do this. I am so proud of you and I love you." Lynelle smiled before she disappeared into the church.

Out of nowhere my father appeared.

"You ready baby?" he asked.

I nodded in agreement, while thinking to myself why the hell everyone keep asking me if I'm ready. I felt like someone was setting me up to get my head chopped off or something. The doors of the church flew open and I felt as if I was gliding towards the front. It was funny. Although I clearly saw Lynelle and my father outside of the church, I could not make out any faces. Everyone was a blur. I didn't understand. I continued my glide towards the altar. I arrived by the side of a tall statue. I began to turn to reveal my future husband....*Rrrrinnnggg.* The phone blared. I tried very hard to ignore it and see my husband.

Rrrriiinnnngg.

"Nnnnoooo," I replied. Upset that I had to get up and answer the phone. I violently pushed the pillows aside and grabbed the phone.

"What!?" I shouted in the phone.

"Oh no. I know you're not talking to me like this," my mom snapped.

"My bad ma. You interrupted my dream," I replied.

"I don't care. It was a dream. Was it that good that you had to yell at the phone like that?" she questioned.

"I was going to see who I was gonna marry." I sighed.

"Gurl, you know it was Rodney. Stop acting like you don't know that. You scared?" she teased.

"No. Mom what you call me for?" I snapped.

"Definitely not to get attitude from you," she snapped back.

"Sorry, Ma. I'm tired," I apologized.

"Uh huh. Anyway. We are having a family dinner at your grandmother's house next Sunday, so if you can try to get off," she asked.

"Okay. I will try," I replied.

"I'll talk to your crabby ass later," my mom teased.

"Ma!"

"Ma, hell! Your attitude is toe up!" My mother laughed.

I laughed and told her I loved her before I hung up the phone. I turned over and looked at the ceiling. I sighed. Closed my eyes and took two deep breaths. I coached myself to get up and prepare to do something. Anything, for the night. I washed my face and brushed my teeth. I walked around my house in my bra and panties, eating cold pizza from two nights ago when the phone rung.

"Hello?"

"Damn, don't you sound like you got a mouth full of balls!" Kim teased.

"Shut up, slut." I laughed, almost spitting the pizza all over.

"Look, what you doing tonight?" Kim asked.

"I don't know. You tell me," she replied.

"Well, let me call Lynelle and see what she wants to do," she stated.

"Cool. Holla back," she yelled before hanging up.

I laughed to myself. And dialed Lynelle.

"Trick. You slept a long time. You sure you ain't pregnant?" she yelled.

"Hi best friend. How are you?" I asked.

"Gurl, I'm chilling."

"What's up for the night Nell?"

"I don't know. It's ladies night at Tony's tonight," Lynelle said happily.

"Tony's' killing me with having his sports bar like a club," I replied.

"Why you get in free!" Lynelle yelled.

"Uh, huh."

"Speaking of free how you and Tony Jr. doing Ms. Playette?" she teased.

"We are just friends Nell. That's all. I have a fiancé, remember. Rodney?!"

"I don't want to hear that. When was the last time he came to see you?" Lynelle questioned.

"Not since the summer started, but he has conditioning for the team," I defended my fiancé.

"Yeah, yeah, yeah whatever. Look, Miss New Car, what time you coming to get me?" she asked.

"Why do I have to drive?" I asked.

"Because you got the fly new sports car," she responded.

"Well, we have to compromise. You come here and I will drive," I demanded.

"Okay. Fine. I'll see you about eight thirty."

"Okay," I agreed.

"Aight. Peace." Lynelle hung up the phone.

I finished my pizza, called Kim to tell her plans and showered. By the time I had finished my shower some one was wildly banging on the door.

"Who da hell?" I said aloud, rushing to my door.

I peeked through the peep hole to see Kim dancing outside of my door. I quickly opened the door.

"Heffa, are you sick? Why are you at the door in your draws?" she shockingly stated while trying to rush inside and close the door to keep the outside from seeing my lace and satin black bra and thong set.

"No, I'm not crazy, but you are, banging on the door like the damn po-lice!" I said, laughing.

"You just nasty. I'mma tell Rod. Watch me...FREAK!" Kim said, rolling her eyes.

"Well, guess what? I learn from the best," I teased.

I rushed to the back to get dressed. I put on my black form fitting J-LO pants, a red J-LO halter top and my red stilettos. I walked into the den to hear Lynelle and Kim discussing the plans for the night.

"Gurl, I can't wait to get to Tony's. I know that fine Torrie gon be there. He is so damn sexy. I been trying to jump his bones since I seen his ass at the beach one night. He got dat new Hummer, too," Lynelle said, smiling.

"And you really trying to ride in that tankard? That's what it is. A big ass tank, looking like he going to war. What war are you fighting in the neighborhood?" Kim laughed.

"The one against all these damn mosquitoes," I interrupted, laughing.

I spun around so that the girls could see my whole outfit.

"Nigga, you ain't fly!" Kim yelled.

"Won't you stop hating on my girl. Lisa, you look real nice. J-LO head to toe, uh?" Lynelle said, coming to my rescue.

"Thanks, girl. My god-sister has always hated on my nice ass and plump boobies," I joked, feeling my body parts.

"Girl, whatever. I'm chill. Everybody ready?" she asked.

"Yeah, you driving?" I slyly asked Kim.

"I could," she replied.

"Well, dammit, let's go," Lynelle squealed.

I always loved riding in Kim's car. She had the brand new Lexus truck. It was black with leather seats and chromed out rims.

"I still don't understand how you get a car like this just working at the bank. I thought tellers didn't make a lot of money?" I quizzed Kim.

"We don't, but that don't mean the general managers don't," Kim responded, hoping around behind the wheel.

"Gurl, shut-up," Lynelle and I yelled in unison.

"What? That nigga got needs and fuck it, I do, too!" Kim defended herself.

"Damn sis, I can't believe it," I said, shaking my head.

"Well, is he at least cute? Ain't GM's usually old?" Lynelle asked.

"Gurl, yes. He's way older than I am, but he is sexy as hell. Like in a Denzel way," Kim stated.

"He won't sexy to me until Training Day. When I looked at the movie I was like DAMN!" I said.

"Gurl, don't you know!" Kim agreed.

By the time we arrived to Tony's we saw the line wrapped around the building.

"You see this shit?" Kim asked.

"Boy, Lisa, I see you working your magic," Lynelle said, looking in disbelief at the long line.

"What you mean by that?" I asked, knowing full well that she meant my connections with Tony Jr.

"Bitch, don't play me," Lynelle replied.

Kim parked and we got out. We walked across the street to stand in when Big Jake recognized me.

"Heeeyyyy, Lisa. Get up here, gurl. You know you don't have to wait, Miss VIP!" he teased, motioning for me and the girls to come through the red velvet roped entrance.

"That's what the hell I'm saying," Kim sang.

We walked to the front and up to the VIP entrance. Kim and Lynelle went through, but Jake stopped me.

"Hey Lisa. Tony is here. He is in y'all spot over in the back of VIP. Take these passes for you and your girls and go surprise that nigga," Jake said.

I nodded as he handed me the passes. I handed the girls their passes and told them that I'd meet them at the table in a minute.

"Yeah, okay. Make sure it is a minute," Kim said with a motherly tone.

"Stop hating!" Lynelle snapped.

She looked at me, smiled and mouthed, "Handle your business."

I mouthed back, "You know I will."

I walked across the VIP section straight to the back where Tony's closed off booth was located with a huge smile.

"What's up with you?" I returned.

"Nothing much. Why didn't you tell me you'd be out?" he said, turning to gaze deep into my eyes.

"Not my idea. It was Kim and Lynelle's idea," I said.

"You don't know how bad I want to kiss you right now," he said.

"So you have a long face for that?" I asked.

"Well, I just—"

Before he could finish I deeply kissed his luscious lips.

"Gonna send y'all a bottle of Moe," Tony said, flashing a smile.

"Good looking," I said, smiling back.

"Can I see you tonight?" he asked.

"Sure, why not?" I replied.

I walked back to the table just in time to order.

"Hey, cutie. You're with these lovely ladies?" the waiter asked.

"I sure am, are you taking our orders?" I flirted with my eyes. I couldn't help but say, "Damn," to myself.

The waiter winked at me while Lynelle and Kim completed their orders.

"And you?" the waiter asked.

I had to admit, she caught me off guard with her joke so much we all were practically falling out of our chairs. Kim quickly stopped her laugh and had a blank stare on her face. Lynelle quickly stopped, too.

"What the hell is wrong with y'all?" Lynelle teased.

"Well, we know you didn't get in here on your own. Miss Ghetto America," David stated.

"Okay, Okay. Let's drop all this. Y'all have a good night. We trying to enjoy ourselves without the drama," Kim interrupted.

"Cool. You ladies have a good night," Anthony said.

David and Anthony walked away. I turned to Lynelle and gave her a stern motherly look.

"What?" Lynelle exclaimed.

"You know what! Why you always gotta start with that boy? Every time we get together, it's the same thing," I fussed

"Just get it over with Nell," Kim said.

"Get what over with?" Lynelle asked.

"Fuck HIM!" Kim and I both replied.

Lynelle began gasping for air and pretending she couldn't breathe.

"Cut that shit, girl. You been wanting David since the first time you met him, why you frontin'?" I asked.

"Ain't nobody fronin' plus—" Before Lynelle could even finish, the waiter arrived with our food.

"Thank GOD…Peace!" I sighed.

"No, Shaun, but if you want to call me Peace, I'll still answer." He laughed.

"So not funny!" Lynelle blabbed.

Kim and I snickered. The waiter placed our food on the table. Asked if we needed anything else and walked away.

"At least he can take a hint." Kim laughed.

The rest of the night we ate and drank and laughed at all the people who thought they were it. I danced with Tony quite a few times. Once I saw Anthony looking at us from the other side of the dance floor. While dancing I wondered what he was thinking but afterwards, Tony made it very clear that he was the only one I were to adore. He swept me off to the private booth with the tinted two way mirrors and doors. He laid me on top of the table and leaned on top of me.

"I saw that dude, staring at us," he whispered in my ear.

"What you talking about?" I asked.

"You know. I don't care who he is, I'm about to show you what he can't do!" He replied.

And with that Tony slowly pulled down my pants and panties and began to devour me like he hadn't eaten all day and I was two piece. He licked and sucked on my clit so much that I couldn't cum anymore. My eyes began to roll in the back of my head and my body started to jerk.

"Shit. I can't do this no more!" I yelled.

"Good thang my booth is sound proof," Tony joked.

"Come on Tony," I seductively pleaded.

"You want me to stop?" he asked.

"No, yes…noooo. Umm, I don't know," I groaned.

"I think I'll let you off the hook, this time."

He said getting up and wiping his mouth with a towel. He pulled me up from the table and cleaned me up. He gave me a huge bear hug and looked into my eyes.

"You know how bad I want you, don't you?" he asked.

"Tony, I know but you know my situation, don't YOU!" I said before walking away.

Chapter 6

Tony returned to his booth thinking about what had just aspired between him and Lisa. He activated the button underneath the table to reveal the flat screen hidden in the opposite side of the booth chair. He loved the way his father allowed him to create his safe haven of a booth. The booth was specially designed and cost his father a quarter of a million dollars. The custom booth was enclosed by double mirror windows, black Italian leather seats. With hidden television he saw Lisa enjoying herself and the way she looked at Anthony made Tony even more upset. Tony wanted Lisa to admire him in that way. He closely studied Lisa and the stranger. He realized a connection between the two. He watched them laugh and enjoy one another. He continued to look when he heard a large bang on the door. Tony quickly pushed the button under the table and waited for the television to disappear behind the cushion of the booth. He opened the door to see his boy Juan standing in front of it.

"What's up, man?" Juan said, giving Tony dap and stepping into the booth.

"Nothing much, man. What's going on?" Tony replied.

"Chilling. Being here in your little booth, I know you seen the flyest girl in the club, haven't you?" Juan asked.

"Naw, man. I've been taking care of the books," Tony lied.

Juan knew Tony had not been tallying the books because he didn't have the calculator and papers all over like he usually does. But he fed in, nonetheless.

"Man she was on the floor dancing, all in to her man. And all the other niggas were wishing they were in her!" Juan joked.

Tony sighed. He didn't want to think about Lisa with another man.

"Word man? How she look?" Tony asked.

"Man she dark, like a chocolate bar, short curly hair. Her skin look smooth as butter. She got some leather pants that BBBOOOOYYY. I can't een explain," Juan said excitedly.

"Well I'll come out there in a few and you show her to me," Tony said.

"Cool. I'll see you in a few," Juan said, catching Tony's hint to leave.

Tony sat down with his head in his hands. He thought about spending time with Lisa. He instantly began to harden.

"Down boy," he said to himself, patting his pants. He stood up, took a deep sigh and walked out of his booth into the noisy club. As soon as he walked out he felt someone grab his behind.

"What the—" Tony said, spinning around to see who violated him. As he turned around, he saw Lisa standing behind him with her arms folded.

"It's about time you came out your bat cave, Mr. Wayne," Lisa teased.

"If you were looking for me, you know how to knock," Tony returned.

"Not your groupie," Lisa stated.

"I know, you my worker," Tony teased.

"Whhaattt!? I got your worker! Believe that," Lisa said and winked.

"Yeah, you do?" Tony replied, licking his lips.

For a moment there was silence, as Tony and Lisa stood staring at each other. Lisa broke the silence.

"Let's dance," Lisa yelled to him while pulling him to the end of the dance floor.

"Buuuttttt. I don't dance. Didn't you see that earlier?" Tony yelled.

"Yeah you do…at least you do tonight," Lisa demanded.

Lisa rushed Tony to the dance floor. Lisa spun Tony around and seductively began dancing in front of him. Tony could not believe how well Lisa danced all over him. In fact, she danced so well that Tony thought she would have been the perfect stripper. Lisa wind her body like a snake slithering on the ground. This made Tony even more curious to find out how she was in bed. He felt she had to be wonderful, the way she made her body twist and turn to the Reggae music. Tony closed his eyes and tried to enjoy the moment. Just as he felt his soldier stand straight as he could in his pants the D.J. interrupted.

"Okay folks, lets take a breather and slow it down a little."

"Oh hell," Tony mumbled.

As soon as Tony grabbed Lisa's hand to walk off the dance floor, Lisa stopped when she heard R. Kelly's voice bellow the beginning lyrics to "It Seems Like Your Ready."

"That's my song," Lisa squealed.

She hopped on Tony, wrapped her legs around his waist and gyrated her hips against his body.

"Hold on," Tony said, trying to balance Lisa.

Lisa hopped down but continued her grind the whole way down.

"This girl has to be mean on a pole," Tony said to himself.

Lisa smiled, hearing what Tony mumbled but, not responding. She continued to grind and sing as the song went on. Others watched from the side as Tony tried to keep up with Lisa's slow grind.

"Look at that girl," Kim said, pulling Lynelle to the side of the dance floor.

"That's my girl!" Lynelle yelled.

Lynelle and Kim were not the only people noticing Lisa's performance, Anthony stood beside a huge pole that separated the dance floor from the lounge area. He thought about all the love making interactions he and Lisa had and became jealous, instantly. Many thoughts began to run across his head. David walked up to Anthony, seeing what Anthony was focusing on. "Damn man, what's up with that?" David asked.

"You know how Lisa is, she likes to dance," Anthony defended Lisa.

"Well looks like ole boy is enjoying her dance quite a bit," David teased.

"I ain't worried. She knows who can work that, OFF the dance floor," Anthony replied.

"Who? Rodney?" David teased again.

"Nigga please. That dude about to be out the picture, little do he know," Anthony said.

"Looks like we got a lot to talk about, cuz," David said patting Anthony on the back.

"Yeah, I do," Anthony said, giving Lisa and Tony one more look before walking out of the club. The two walked pass Kim and Lynelle on the way out. Kim stopped Anthony.

"You gone, bro?" Kim asked.

"Yeah, I'm gone. Tell your sister when she finish getting her groove on, to give me a call," Anthony sarcastically replied.

"Will do," Kim said.

Lynelle watched Anthony and David, especially David, walk out of the club. Once she could no longer see the guys she turned to Kim.

"Damn gurl, Anthony looked hurt," Lynelle slowly said.

"Yeah, I know, Lisa got all these men falling over her and shit and look at us." Kim pouted.

"Speak for yourself. I'm about to show David a few things," Lynelle snapped.

"What about cha man?" Kim asked.

"What he don't know, won't hurt him," Lynelle responded.

"Oh Lawd!" Kim playfully held her hands towards the sky, yelling.

The girls were having so much fun they did not notice Tony and Lisa walk up. Lisa was fanning herself with her hand.

"Bitch you ought to be fanning, out there dancing like you at Magic City and poor Tony is your pole!" Lynelle teased.

Lisa just smiled. Tony did the same.

"Well ladies I am retiring for the night. Your girl here has tired me out," Tony said, hugging Lisa.

"Okay, you have a nice night," Kim said.

Lisa turned to Tony, stood on the tips of her toes and placed her lips so close to Tony's ear that the hair on the back of his neck stood up from the sensation.

"Thank you for a lovely night. I really enjoyed myself," Lisa whispered.

Tony picked her up and returned the favor.

"No problem. I hope I can see you soon, other than in the club," he said.

He placed her back on the floor, bend over her, hugged her tight and then kissed her forehead. He turned around and looked at Kim and Lynelle.

"You ladies cool? You need any more to drink or eat?" he questioned.

"No, we're cool. Thanks, Tony," Lisa quickly responded before Kim or Lynelle could open their mouths.

"Okay, if you need anything, send Lisa. The boys know she's my special friend and they will put it all on my tab," Tony announced before walking off.

"How you speaking for us?" Lynelle asked Lisa.

"Because we're about to bounce," Lisa returned.

Kim quickly followed suit. "Yeah, I'm tired and I have to go to work in the morning.

"Aaaalllright," Lynelle finally agreed.

As the girls walked out of the building, Lisa stopped at the corner.

"Did y'all see where Anthony went?" she asked.

"Yeah, he said to tell you to call him," Kim relayed the message.

"Yeah in so many words," Lynelle replied.

Lisa had a feeling what that meant, so she did not respond. The ride to Lisa's house was very silent. Even once they arrived to Lisa's apartment and departed their separate ways. Everyone let out a dry, "See ya later," and left. Lisa went inside and immediately took a shower. The hot steamy water gave her enough time to think about the night's events. It also gave her more than enough time to sit and wonder why Anthony left without saying goodbye.

"Closing time. Y'all ain't got to go home, but y'all got's to get the hell outta here," The D.J. announced through the mic.

Tony was sitting in his booth watching the crowd depart. Once he saw the last person leave, he gathered all his things, locked them in the safe under the seat and headed towards the door.

"Hey boss, you want me to lock up?" Trent yelled from behind the bar.

"Yeah man, I'm tired as hell," Tony replied.

"You should be. I seen that thick chick working you over," Trent joked.

"Yeah, man, she got me," Tony admitted as he walked out the door.

"I can't believe Lisa was dancing like that with that nigga," Anthony said to David.

"Yo man, ever since you came back in town you been real sensitive when it comes Lisa. What's up with that?" David asked.

"Man, I can't keep my mind off of her. It's like I made a big ass mistake. I mean, I love J and Ri, but I'm not in love with Ri. Man, I ain't gone eva love nobody like I love Lisa. She my heart. I been loving her since we were kids," Anthony said, leaning his head back on the seat.

David kept driving, but felt his pain just from the tone of his voice. Anthony took a deep sigh and continued.

"Me and Lisa slept together," Anthony confessed and waited for David's response. Silence became thick and Anthony couldn't take it any longer.

"Did you hear what I said?" Anthony asked.

"Yeah man, I hear you, but that ain't no big news. Man I knew once you came back home it would be just a matter of time. We all knew that. Damn man, Maria knows how much you love Lisa. I mean besides the point that your dumb ass told her!"

They both laughed and David continued.

"You gotta think about what you want to do. Yeah, you love Lisa and that is all good, but you got a wife and a kid, man. You have to decide what is more important," David said.

David stopped at the entrance of Anthony's apartment complex.

"You going home tonight or you going to the pad and think about some shit?" David asked.

"I'm going to the pad," Anthony said slowly.

David took his cell phone out of the cup holder and called Maria. Anthony laid the seat down so far that he was almost touching the back seat.

"Yo Maria, what's up? This David. Anthony gonna stay with me tonight. He kinda messed up and I don't feel like driving his drunk ass home this late," David explained to Maria.

There was silence.

"Oh, okay. I'll let him know that. Aight. Peace." David hung up the phone.

"What she say?" Anthony asked.

"She told me to tell you she and Mal are going to her moms," David said, relaying the message.

"See man that's another thang. She always talking about she going to D.C. Her ass ain't ever here wit my son. For all I know she fucking some otha nigga," Anthony said.

"Well, that's the shit you need to think about. You knew y'all had an agreement. You should have thought about everything before you let that girl have yo baby. I mean think about it, Kid. She knew about you and Lisa and she still had your kid and you still married her. What kindda chick gonna marry a man, knowing good and well that dude in love with somebody else?" David looked over at Anthony.

David started driving again until her reached a stop light. Anthony looked out the window.

"I know, but I wanted a baby so bad man. Everyone on base had kids or was about to. They told me how much money they got extra and all that shit. Maria knew I wanted a baby," Anthony pleaded.

"Yeah, now look at her. Don't want to work, always in D.C. You don't know what she doing. You have to ask yourself, do you really want to be like this? What is good for Jamaal? You betta hope she don't be having him around no otha nigga," David exclaimed.

"Yeah man, I know," was all Anthony could get out.

David arrived at their bachelor pad. The two men got out of the car and headed to the door. Anthony reached the door first. He took out his key and headed straight to his room. He passed Daniel on the way to the back of the townhouse.

"Hey. What's up wit you?" Daniel said stopping his cousin at the bathroom beside the steps.

"The usual. I'm just glad us three decided to buy this house, for damn nights like this," Anthony said, walking up the steps going straight to his room. David followed.

"Yo, what's wrong wit dat nigga?" Daniel asked pointing up the steps in the direction Anthony disappeared to.

"He saw Lisa tonight at Tony's and his mind gone...the usual," David said, smiling.

"Damn. He need to get his hoes straight," Daniel joked.

"Who the hell you telling?" David joined in.

"She have her girls wit her?" Daniel asked.

"Yeah, Lynelle and Kim," David said.

"Kim fine. Thick ass Lynelle still trying to fuck?" Daniel asked.

"Yeah, I'mma still hang her for a little while thought. Make her really want a nigga. I'm out, though. I'm tired as hell," David said, yawning.

"I hear ya. I just want to get wit Kim for a night. To see what's up," Daniel said.

"Boy that ain't even nice to be fucking the whole crew," David said, walking up the steps.

"It ain't nice, but it'll feel good," Daniel said, following.

"Y'all some guppies," Anthony yelled from the closed door.

"Betta a guppie than a yuppie, you love sick bitch!" David yelled back.

Daniel laughed uncontrollably as he walked into his room. He and David closed their doors in unison.

"Fuck y'all!" Anthony shouted.

"Yelp!" Daniel yelled.

"Both y'all shut the hell up and go to sleep. Y'all betta be in church tomorrow. Bastards," David yelled.

The three guys laughed and suddenly the whole house fell silent. Moments later David began to snore loudly.

"Damn. I knew I should have went to sleep first," Daniel said.

"That's what's up," Anthony replied.

Everyone in the house were asleep soon after Anthony's statement. Not worrying about what the morning had awaiting them when they rouse.

Chapter 7

The sun was glaring through the blinds of my bedroom making me regret having to face the day. Not knowing what I was going to have to face when I got home to Maria, I laid in the bed trying to keep my eyes closed as long as possible. Concentrating on what I was going to tell Maria, I heard my cell phone buzzing, indicating that I have a text message. I looked at the clock on the phone and it read 8:45am. I pushed the button to display the message.

> Good morning. I know you probably
> drunk too much last night, but
> You going to church?

I read the message again then looked at the sender, although I really did not need to, I knew Maria could be the only one to send the message. No one else would be worrying about me like that. She always wanted to pretend that we were this happy go lucky couple. She and I both knew the truth. I decided to text her back.

Good morning to you, too. Yeah, I
Was a little messed up. I'm
Chill now, You know I will be in
Church. I have clothes here.

"Why you tell her that?" I said to myself. I knew that would lead to a full blown out conversation. As I had predicted, the phone rang. I took a deep breath and answered.

"Yeah, what's up?" I answered.

"Dang, is that the way you talk to your wife?" she responded.

"What's up RiRi? What's the deal?"

"Nothing. I was making Jamaal breakfast and I decided to call you to see if you were going to church. I didn't know if you'd be awake so I decided to text you instead," she explained.

"Oh well, I'm gonna go and get ready. I'll see you sometime this afternoon," I said, trying to get her off the phone.

"Okay. Jamaal and I won't be going to church. We're about to head out."

"Head out? Where the hell y'all going on Sunday?" I questioned.

"We have a play date with Devonna and her kids today."

"Oh, okay. Tell home girl I said what's up."

There was a pause as I thought about her "play date."

"RiRi?" I called into the phone, with a perplexed look on my face.

"Yeah baby, what's up?" Maria answered.

"I thought Devonna lived in D.C. near your peoples?" I asked.

"She came down last night to see her friend so we gonna hang out until she leaves to go back," she replied.

I sat on the phone for a while and thought about everything. Something sound funny. I decided to leave it alone for the moment.

"Y'all have fun then. I'll see you later," I said.

"Okay. I love you," she replied.

"I love you, too," I returned.

I placed the phone on the pillow, but not before I glanced at the sign 9:45 am. "I talked to that girl for an hour?" I said to myself.

I turned over and closed my eyes. As soon as I began to think about Lisa and that dude on the dance floor, my door flew open.

"Yo niggga, get up!" David yelled.

"Why? What is wrong with you?" I said, wondering why he had burst through my door like he saw a ghost.

"Man I was looking at ESPN right?"

I nodded in agreement.

"And I saw that, that dude Rodney got picked up by the Rebels," he announced.

I sat on the edge of the bed. I knew I had a blank look on my face because David responded to the silence.

"I know man. That's some shit. I knew nigga was alright in high school but I heard he was garbage in college."

I got myself together and finally responded.

"That's good for him," was all I could manage to get out.

David shook his head as he walked out of the room. I sat in silence wondering if my chance with Lisa was gone knowing that she was about to be a real rich lady.

"What!? I can't believe it. Are you serious?" I yelled in the phone.

"Yeah, baby I got the phone call early this morning. And news hit fast because I was looking at ESPN and it scrolled across the screen. I'm so happy right now! My moms and pops are popping bottles and shit. It's wild!" Rodney shouted.

"I'm so proud of you baby. That's good. You deserve it. Why didn't you tell me your camp you were in was a pro-ball camp? You had me thinking you were at the school," I said.

"Thanks baby. I wanted it to be a surprise. Are you?" he replied.

"Yes baby. I am surprised and excited for you," I said.

"You should be excited for us!" he said.

"Well, you will be the one on the field and stuff. I'll just be another adoring fan!" I replied.

"Look, enough of all the chit chat. Put some clothes on, I'm coming to get you in an hour. Bye," he quickly said, hanging up the phone.

I placed the phone on the table and hurried to the bathroom. The whole time not believing what I had just heard. All this time Rodney has been away trying out for a professional foot ball team. I just could not believe it. I pulled out a pair of hazel contacts from the medicine cabinet, I had to look extra cute, regular ones just would not do. And now that my fiancé would be making the big bucks, all the more reason to bring out the special occasion eyes! I ran into my room took out a pair of black Baby Phat slacks and a lace Baby Phat purple blouse. It was a good thing I had already taken a bath or there would have been no way I would have been ready in one hour. Rodney know perfection of beauty takes time! I grabbed my purple pumps from my shoe tree and headed back to the bathroom to make last preparations before Rodney came. As I was gliding the second coat of grapefruit lip gloss across my lips, Rodney was knocking at the door. I slowly walked to the door. I wanted him to be taken by appearance. I stopped two feet from the know reached over and opened the door. The pause told me everything. There was silence before he actually spoke.

"Oh my DAMN!" he said, staring me up and down. I smiled and waited for him to come in. I had not seen Rodney in about two months. And he was looking even better than before. His arms and legs were large and he even had a natural glow. I guess money can make anything light up! Look at me. I was running around like I had just won the lottery.

"Baaabbbyyy. You look good. DAMN baby, I know I have not seen you in a couple of months, but you've changed," he said excitedly.

"Well, are you gonna come in and see me or what?" I asked, pulling him inside of the house.

Rodney walked in, closed the door and gave me a big bear hug.

"You gonna wrinkle my clothes and I don't even know where we are going," I said, trying to pull away.

"Ah, come on, baby. I haven't seen you," he said.

He continued to hug me, smelling my hair and neck.

"You smell so good. You feel good too, Hump."

"Hump what?" I asked.

"I want you," he said, feeling on my ass and caressing my back.

"Rod, don't we have to go somewhere?" I asked.

"Yeah, but that can wait. I want you now!" he whispered.

I could not front. I wanted him too, but he had to want me more that way I knew he'd do me just right. I played with him for a little while.

"Rod, I just got dressed. I want to look perfect and fresh when you take me where we are going," I pleaded.

He began to beg, like I knew he would.

"Come on, baby. I got to have your sweet pussy. Please let me taste you," he begged.

"Fine," I said, pretending as if he had persuaded me to be in on his sexual game.

He picked me up by the hips, I wrapped my legs around his waist and we headed to the bedroom. He laid me on the bed, took off my pumps and slide my pants over my feet.

"Mmmm, you look sooo damn good!" he said as he pulled my black sheer thongs over my feet like he did the pants. My body tingled all over as I waited anxiously for Rodney to satisfy my body. He rubbed his massive hands across my warm wet pussy. I trembled. He caressed me until I begged for more.

"C'mon, Rod. Stop teasing me. Taste me," I asked.

"Say please," he teased.

"Please, baby, Please taste me," I begged.

Without hesitation, he slowly licked around my warm mound. I almost lost control completely, but I wasn't wiggling like he wanted me to. He took his right hand, separated my lips and ate me like he never had before. I was all over the bed trying to run away. Every time I would scoot away, he would pull me closer to him. He did not stop until I came so hard that I was halfway off the bed.

"Baby, where are you going?" Rodney laughed.

"That's not funny, you did that on purpose. You trying to get me caught up," I said.

"Ah, come here, baby," Rodney teased while lifting me up.

He pulled my shirt over my head and unhooked my bra.

"What are you doing? Why are you undressing me when you are fully clothed?" I asked.

"Oh, don't worry, you won't be alone," he said.

In a flash it seemed Rodney was completely naked.

"You feel better?" he asked with a smile.

"Yeess, much better." I smiled back.

Rodney laid beside me. I looked at him with a perplexed look.

"What?" he teased.

"You got me naked and sticky to lay beside me naked?" I asked.

He pulled me on top of him. At that time I knew what time it was. I straddled him and began to work him over.

"Damn baby. What in the hell? You missed me like that Boo?" he groaned.

"Yeah, Daddy, I missed you. Let me show you just how much!" I said.

As I bounced up and down I nibbled and licked on his nipples. He groaned and moaned. He cupped my ass with his hands and guided my body up and down his manhood.

"Damn, Lisa, you feel so good," he groaned.

"Do I?" I asked.

"Yeah, baby. Make Daddy cum," he begged.

"Oh, I will," I responded.

I bounced faster and higher as he groaned and moaned.

"I'm about to c—uumm," he shouted.

"You mean you came!" I teased.

"You funny. Don't play, gurl. You know how you make me feel," he said between breaths.

I wiped the sweat from his forehead and then kissed it. I laid on the bed as Rodney cupped my body and whispered," I Love You."

"I Love you, too. Now don't we have somewhere to go?" I asked, looking into his eyes.

He looked down at his watch and jumped up.

"Oh shit. We gotta go," he screamed, scrambling for clothes.

"Don't we have to take showers first? I'm not going no where smelling like hot sex!" I yelled at him.

"Fine, baby. Go shower. I'll join you in a minute," he said.

I headed to the bathroom to shower, but not before watching Rodney grab his cell and head to the front of the apartment. In the middle of my shower Rodney came into the bathroom. He pulled the shower curtain back and stepped in.

"Damn, gurl. You make me want to say forget where we have to go and just stay here and play with you for the rest of the day," he said, smiling.

"Play? That's what you do with me? Play?" I asked.

"Baby, you know what I mean! I'm just playing," he recanted.

"You better rephrase that!" I said playfully.

"See you playing too much!" he yelled from the room. I put on a brand new pair of under clothes and put back on my Baby Phat outfit. I walked around the house shoeless until Rodney dressed. I laid on the couch and waited for Rodney. While I waited, Rodney's phone began to buzz. I sat there wondering if I should just let it buzz or see what the buzzing was about. I decided to let it buzz. Rodney walked out dressed and smelling good.

"You ready Baby?" he asked.

"Yeah. Your phone was ringing," I said, sliding into my pumps.

"Oh yeah?" he asked, picking up the phone.

He pushed a few buttons and paused for a moment. The he laughed. He headed to the door and opened it.

"You coming?" he asked.

"Yeah, what's so funny?" I asked, following him out.

"Nothing," he responded.

The ride was pretty quiet until I saw where we were pulling into.

"You made me get up and dressed and stop cuddling to go to Tony's?" I asked.

He remained quiet. Totally quiet not saying a word. I just looked. For it to be one o'clock in the afternoon, the place was packed. I figured a big game was coming on, like the Cowboys playing the Redskins or something like that. The Rebels couldn't have a game on because Rodney was with me. And then I thought, it couldn't be a pro-football game yet. It was only the end of July. It was obvious that Rodney wasn't going to tell me what was up so I waited for him to park. Once we got out the car and began walking to the entrance, I stopped and turned to Rodney.

"Baby. What is going on?" I confusedly asked.

He took me by the hand, kissed me on my forehead and pulled me closer to the door. As soon as he opened the door the whole building was full of cheers, applause and happiness. I couldn't help but smile instantly. Rodney and I receiving all that attention excited me. A very tall gray haired man walked up to us and grabbed Rodney's hand.

"Congratulations, baby boy. I'm so proud of you. I knew you could do it." The man hugged him and then looked at me.

"Ah, is this Lisa? She is so beautiful. You did good, son. Damn, you did good," the man said, looking at me up and down and smiling.

"Thanks, Granddad. Lisa this is my granddad. My mom's dad. He came here from North Carolina," Rodney said, introducing me.

"Nice to meet you, sir," I said, smiling.

"My pleasure, doll. My pleasure," he said, almost refusing to let my hand go.

"Okay, Granddad. Let her go." Rodney laughed.

His granddad released my hand and walked away smiling.

"Let's go, baby," Rodney said, removing me from my spot.

We walked over to a huge table decorated and placed in the middle of the dance floor. Our parents and closest friends were sitting at the table with two empty chairs in the middle. Everyone were smiling and once we sat down I leaned over to Rodney and whispered in his ear.

"What is going on?" I demanded to know.

"SSShhh," he whispered back.

Out of nowhere Tony appeared with a mic and stood in the middle of the floor.

"Thank you all for coming out for this special event. I have to admit when I received the call from Rodney's parents asking to rent out the lounge in such short notice I panicked. But for those of you who know Rodney's mother know she handled it all. She was here at seven in the morning commanding and pointing. And needless to say, my men were moving," Tony said.

Laughter filled the room. Along with quite a few "I know that's right" and "That's her."

Tony continued. "I would like to say thank you for choosing my establishment for your even and hopefully you won't be disappointed," he said, turning to face our table. For a second our eyes locked and then he snapped back.

"Well, lets not prolong the celebration. As some of you may have heard, I would like to introduce the new starting running back to some and present to others, the new member of the Virginia Rebels. Rodney Running Man Taylor." The building, once again, broke into a loud roar. I joined in. Rodney got up from his seat and walked over to Tony. They gave each other dap and Tony handed Rodney the microphone.

"Thank you. Man. Y'all know everything Tony said about my mom is right," he said, turning to look at his mom and blowing her a kiss before continuing.

"But I love her though. I want to thank all of y'all for coming out and celebrating this time with me. But before I go on I have to say, I am not taking this experience alone. I would like to thank my fiancé, Lisa, for dealing with me through camp and all. Let me tell y'all, she did not know I was in pro camp. She thought I was back at school conditioning for the upcoming college season. I love you Baby. We gone make this happen," he said, looking at me. All the attention made me blush. I guess he noticed because he turned back around began to speak.

"I won't embarrass her too much. She knows how much I love her. Anyway I want to thank everyone for supporting me. I want to thank Tony for allowing us to have his place at such short notice and I am sure we won't be disappointed by anything today. I told my mom once I found out about being placed on the team that I wanted to have one big celebration with my friends and family before I buckle down and start the season. And believe it or not…well I'm pretty sure you'll all believe that momma put this all together by herself. I'm not gonna talk y'all heads off, but before I introduce Coach Tallwood, I would like to thank all of you for coming and fulfilling my wish of everyone being together. Without further hindrance from me, Coach Tallwood."

Rodney handed his head coach the mic and returned to his seat. Rodney's coach began to speak about how special he knew Rodney was and how important he was to the team. All I really heard was, "Yadda yadda yadda," as I survived the room and everyone in it. Bust in the midst of the yadda yaddas I almost choked on the statement that Coach Tallwood said. It went something like, "And I am pretty sure Rodney's wife to be would love the fact that he just signed a fifteen point five million dollar contract with a one point five million dollar signing bonus."

I almost died choking on my tea. I watch as Coach Tallwood handed Rodney a piece of paper. I looked at Rodney. He smiled. As Coach Tallwood continued to talk, I waited for everyone's attention to be off the main table and back on the coach, who was explaining the teams schedule and how it would effect local businesses and the population. I leaned over to Rodney and whispered in his ear

"Is all of this true?"

"As true as the sky is blue…well on some days," he joked.

He leaned over and kissed me. He whispered in my ear again.

"This paper he gave me, it is only that paper. The one point five is already in the bank. I have one million in my account and I opened up an account with only your name on it. It has the point five in it."

I looked at him with my eyes popping out.

"I'm not finished. Every month point five will go into your account, point five will go into a joint account that I want you to use for bills. And the rest will go into my account. I told you I'd always take care of you. I love you and always will. Now I'm finished," he said, kissing my once more wiping the tears from my face that I had not noticed had fallen.

By this time, Coach Tallwood had completed his extra long speech and had sat down. One of the waiters from the lounge had come to the middle of the floor to announce that lunch would be served in a moment. Everyone began to mingle. I was still in shock from what Rodney had just disclosed.

"I'll be right back, baby, I'm going to mingle a little," he said.

I nodded to let him know I had heard him, but continued to sit. I was staring into space when I was hugged from behind.

"Hey, guurrllll!" Kim and Lynette yelled.

"Oh my GOD. I did not know y'all was here!" I screamed.

"Miss Ghetto wanted to scream at you when you and Rod walked in, but I covered her mouth!" Lynelle teased.

"Stop playing, you know that was her," Kim protested.

We gave each other a few more hugs and kisses and I told them we'd be meeting tonight at my house because Rodney was flying out to Atlanta tonight. They agreed. Lynelle bent down and whispered in my ear.

"We need to talk. Alone. I know we do. I see it in your face," Lynelle said.

I told her okay and she pushed Kim back to their seats. Lynelle always knew me. Knew what I was thinking and for the most part how I felt. She always had the ability to see right through me. I knew what she wanted to talk to me about. I enjoyed the rest of the afternoon eating shrimp, lobster, steak and other expensive foods and drinking expensive drinks. I could not even imagine how much money Rod spent on this so called celebration. I barely spent any time with him at Tony's. He spent much of his time mingling and laughing it up with the people. By the end of the party, I was tired and ready to go home.

"Hey beautiful, you ready to leave?" Rodney asked, helping me up from the table.

"Boy am I ever. Baby, I am so damn tired it ain't even funny," I said.

"Well let's go. What happened to your parents?" Rodney asked.

"They left, daddy was tired," I lied.

I didn't have the nerve to tell him that daddy just didn't like him and that he got tired of him flaunting and made mom take him home.

"Well, let's go," Rodney said, putting his arm around me.

Rodney yelled goodbye to everyone and we left.

Chapter 8

Church was good. I needed it. I found it mighty ironic though when the preacher stated that the title of his sermon was "The other side of Love." I felt like he was talking about me but just flipped it to a spiritual meaning. He talked about being caught between the love of GOD and the world. He used just about every worldly love he could, from alcohol to drugs to someone's spouse. I kept saying to myself, "He has to be talking about me." On the way home, I thought about everything Rev said. I couldn't help but think about me and Lisa. I loved her so much I stopped at the local pier to contemplate on some things before I went home to hear Maria's mouth. I sat for a while, thinking about what I'm gonna do about my situation. My cousins were all about having Maria and Lisa, but I couldn't. Every time I think about Lisa with another man, I get so pissed. And I know since that nigga Rodney signed that contract, he will be taking her away. If he's smart he will. I know I would. I left when the thought of Lisa leaving, after I fought so hard to get orders back home, began to make me madder than ever.

I took a deep sigh to prepare for Maria's mouth and walked through the door.

"Daadddy," Jamaal yelled, rushing towards me.

"Hey, buddy. What's up?" I asked.

I hugged and kissed him before I placed him back on the floor to run off to the back of the apartment. I walked through the living room and saw Maria in the kitchen cooking.

"What's up?" I asked.

"Hey, baby. Nothing, just cooking some greens, pork chops, macaroni and cheese with a little sweet potato pudding on the side."

I walked in, looked over the stove at all the food, sniffed and looked at her.

"What got into you? Cooking and stuff. Do I need some antacid or something? You didn't put laxative in it did you?" I joked.

"Stop playing. Me and my baby gotta eat this food!" she smiled.

I grabbed her by the waist, turned her around and planted a huge kiss on her lips. She stopped the kiss, looked at me and stroked my face in such a gentle way I almost forgot about Lisa and everything that came with her. We continued our kiss for about two more minutes before she remembered that she was cooking.

"Boy. What you trying to do? You gonna make me burn all this good food," she said, pushing me aside to continue cooking.

I smacked her on her ass and walked away.

"Ouch Boy! Don't make me hurt you," she yelled from the kitchen.

"Hurt me, Momma! Hurt me!" I yelled back.

"Hurt me, Mommy," Jamaal yelled, trying his best to mock me.

I laughed and for once actually felt food about being home with my wife. I laid across the bed to rest before I filled my belly with all the food that Maria was cooking.

RRiiinnngggg. Rrriiinnnnggg.

"Anthony are you gonna get that?" Maria yelled from the kitchen.

The phone continued to ring she grabbed a towel to clean her hands before answering the phone.

"Hello?"

"What took you so long to answer the phone? You ova there giving my pussy away?" the voiced asked.

Maria quietly rushed to the bedroom to see Anthony laying across the bed fast asleep. She returned to the kitchen whispering into the phone.

"Devonna, are you crazy call me asking dumb shit like that? Anthony is here in the other room," Maria hissed into the phone.

"My bad. Whatcha getting mad for, his doggish ass would probably just ask if he could join. Damn men. They in sensitive like that shit," Devonna said.

"Well, I don't want you calling talking like that," Maria pleaded.

"You liked me talking like that earlier when I was eating you out! I don't get it. You need to leave that nigga. What good is it for you to cry to me because he's telling you he still love his ex but you stay? I don't understand," Devonna lectured.

"You just don't understand. I Love him," Maria replied.

"But do he love you? See, that's what I'm talking about. Men are so dumb. They don't know how to cater to a woman's needs. They not sensitive, scared to be or they too sensitive and want to be us!" Devonna said.

Maria let out a faint laugh.

"See that's what I'm talking about baby girl. I'm not fussing or mad at you. I just want you to be happy. If you be with me, you don't have to worry about who I love," Devonna responded.

"I know I can't right now though. I want what's best for Jamaal and he wouldn't understand why Auntie Devonna and Mommy are sleeping in the same bed, kissing and shit," Maria said.

"I won't wait the rest of my life Maria, I have a heart, too," Devonna said.

"I know. I know," Maria whispered.

"I'm gone. I'll hit you on the cell later since the part-time husband is back," Devonna said as she hung up the phone.

Maria did not even say goodbye. She hung up the phone and completed her meal wondering how long she had to lead a double life. Often the question of her sexuality ran through her mind, but Devonna bought things to light that she had not before. She thought about all the times that she was kissed tenderly or caressed and pleased with out giving directions. And every time, Devonna had bought that joy and tenderness to her life. Devonna always made her feel like the only woman in the world and with Devonna she didn't have to compete with anyone else.

"Damn," Maria said painfully.

"Damn what?" Anthony asked, standing in the entrance of the kitchen. Maria jumped and grabbed the plates before they hit the floor.

"Ant. You scared the shit out of me," Maria gasped, placing the plates on the counter and breathing deeply.

"My bad. Damn What?" Anthony asked again.

"I needed to wash clothes," Maria lied.

"Oh yeah, 'cause I only got one uniform left. You gonna do that tonight?" Anthony asked.

"Yeah," Maria replied slowly.

"You made biscuits too. You on point today gurl," Anthony said, grabbing a biscuit from the pan as Maria pulled it out of the oven. He had not noticed the pain in Maria's face instead headed towards the den.

"Let me know when the food done," he yelled, walking out.

Maria agreed and began placing food on individual plates. Once she had prepared plates for herself, Anthony and Jamaal, she called them to the table. Anthony rushed into the dining room and grabbed the plate and drink off the table.

"Thanks, baby," Anthony said, attempting to return to the den.

"Ant. I was thing—"

Before Maria could complete her statement, Anthony had darted to the den, sat down and began watching television.

"You say something, Ri?" Anthony yelled from the den.

"No," Maria quietly lied.

She turned towards her son and tried to smile best as she could, but deep inside her heart ached. She and Jamaal ate silently in the dinning room while Anthony enjoyed his dinner in the den.

After dinner Maria cleared the table and cleaned the kitchen. She gave Jamaal a bath and put him to sleep. She walked into her bedroom and saw Anthony laying across the bed.

"Are you going anywhere?" Maria asked.

"No, why?" Anthony responded.

"Because I'm gonna go out with Devonna to the club," Maria replied.

"On a Sunday?" he asked.

"Yeah," she said.

"Oh, aight. When will you be back?" he asked.

"I don't know. It ain't like I gotta job to go to tomorrow," Maria sarcastically said.

"Ump, that's by choice," Anthony said.

"Whatever," Maria said, walking to the closet to take out clothes to put on.

Maria continued her procedure with out saying a word to Anthony. Once she was fully dressed, Maria walked to the door and yelled, "Don't wait up," before walking out and closing the door.

"I won't," Anthony replied under his breath, but Maria did not hear him.

Maria walked out to her car and called Devonna on her cell phone.

"Hello?" Devonna sounded surprised to hear Maria on the other end.

"Hey, can we meet somewhere?" Maria asked.

"You mean Mr. I'm not concerned is staying home long enough to keep Jamaal so you can be out alone?" Devonna asked.

"Not now, can you see me or not?" Maria said.

"I'm sorry, you know I'll meet you. Just say where," Devonna recanted.

"I don't know," Maria said.

"Why don't you come over here to the crib?" Devonna asked.

"What if someone sees me? Then Anthony might find out that you live her and not in D.C.," Maria said.

"Who gonna know I stay thirty minutes away from you, in the white folks section. Nobody knows that nigga round here," Devonna pleaded.

"Okay," Maria gave in.

"I'll see you in about thirty?" Devonna asked.

"Yeah. See ya," Maria said, hanging up the phone.

Maria drove as fast as she could crying the whole way. She did not understand why Anthony did not care about her like she wanted him to. She took care of him and even had a baby for him when no one else would. She thought about all the times Lisa would call Anthony and how upset he would be because she would not have his baby. Maria remembered that night vividly. Anthony cried and yelled. He told her how much he loved Lisa but she had a boyfriend. He kept saying he'd never loved anyone like her before. That night she promised herself that she would give Anthony the love that he longed for. She deeply felt that she could give him the love he wanted from Lisa. She remembers holding him tight, rubbing his head and telling him everything would be alright. She gently kissed him and wiped his face. She straddled Anthony and starting kissing him more. She remembers Anthony stopping her and telling that they shouldn't be doing that because they were just friends and he loved Lisa. "Don't worry I will always be your friend. Don't friends help each other out? I don't want to see you hurt. I want to love you and give you what you want, no strings," were Maria's exact words. Maria deeply sighed thinking about those words. She continued think about that night. She undressed Anthony and slowly sucked and teased his body all over. Then she undressed and made love to Anthony like she never had to anyone else before. She even remember Anthony trying to use a condom and she told him no. When Anthony was about to cum, she wrapped her legs around his waist clamping a strong hold on him. Anthony had no choice but to explode inside of her. They both were so exhausted that night that they fell asleep right where they were. Nine and a half months later, she had Jamaal.

Maria looked up and had noticed that she had arrived to Devonna's house. She parked and walked up to the door. Devonna opened the door and stepped back.

"Damn. You look horrible. What the hell is up?" Devonna said grabbing Maria's arm and pulling her into the house. Maria wiped her face and sat on the couch.

"I was just thinking about the night Anthony and I conceived Jamaal, after Lisa told him she wouldn't have a baby for him," Maria said.

"What about it?" Devonna asked.

"Just that he was so gentle and shit that night and now he just don't care about my at all," Maria cried.

"Look Baby Gurl, you shouldn't be crying. You made a mistake. We all do. You just need to learn from it," Devonna said.

"I didn't make a mistake. I knew what I was doing. I loved...love him. Why can't he see that?" Maria cried loudly.

"Maybe because love is blind and you both are acting like Ray and Stevie on a damn tour. You both want to give what you want, hear what you want, but can't see shit!" Devonna said.

"What do you mean?" Maria asked.

"Look, for real you can't be mad at him. He told you that he loved someone else. But you was blind because you like him so much. He was blind because he was actually dumb enough to ask someone who had a boyfriend, to have his baby. Now both of you are together thinking that it would change but he's only comparing you to her. And you just mad-" Devonna paused.

"What? Speak your peace," Maria begged.

"Well, it ain't peaceful, it's the truth and although I don't want to hurt you, you need to hear it. I just don't know if it's the right time or not," Devonna said.

"Just say it," Maria yelled.

"Fine. You just made because you ain't her. You want that nigga so bad, you want to be her," Devonna blurted out.

The room was silent. Devonna starred at Maria for a reaction. Two minutes later two tears rolled down Maria's face as she stood up.

"You know, you right. From now on I'm gonna be me," Maria sternly said, pointing to herself.

"And who the hell are ya?" Devonna joked.

Maria sat down and thought.

"I'm Maria, damn it! I don't know why I'm married because I've been bi-sexual since damn twelfth grade," Maria announced.

"Hold on!" Devonna screamed.

"You mean you been licking and getting the sticking since then?" Devonna teased.

"Bitch, don't play. You knew that," Maria said.

"Well, why don't Ant know?" Devonna asked.

Maria sat down and placed her head in her hands.

"Because when I went to the military, I thought I changed. I saw Anthony and I knew he'd make me the woman my parents wanted me to be," she said.

Devonna removed her hands, looked deeply into her eyes and asked, "But what kind of woman does Maria want to be?"

81

Maria looked at Devonna and hugged her.

"You always want what's best for me," she said.

"Why should I want anything less? How can my life prosper if I don't help others and wish them good?" Devonna replied.

"I am so confused. I love Jamaal. I love Anthony, but I love you, too," Maria said.

Devonna's eyes opened wide. She sat down beside Maria and hugged her.

"You do?" she asked.

"Yes, I've had a crush on you since senior year," Maria disclosed.

"So why didn't yo say anything?" Devonna asked.

"Because I've heard so many people say how same sex relationships weren't right. How those people would go to hell. I did not want to be apart of the hatred. I didn't want to disappoint anyone," Maria said.

"You mean, you go to church and don't understand that GOD loves everyone?"

Before Maria could answer, she continued.

"And disappoint anyone? So you rather disappoint yourself and feel bad so that others can feel good? And let me not forget about being hated. You got haters everywhere. I mean damn Ri, look how many people hated Jesus, Bill Gates and all these otha people who rose to the occasions and you worried about these little people around here?" Devonna said.

"Gurl please. You really gotta get your shit together," Devonna shouted.

"You right. I have a lot to think about. I understand that. Maybe I should to away," Maria said.

"Go away? You can't run from your problems," Devonna said.

"I don't mean run away, I just want time to think about my life and what I want to do," Maria responded.

Devonna leaned over to Maria, kissed her on her cheek and held her tight. The rest of the night Devonna and Maria watched movies and cuddled until the wee hours of the morning, before Maria returned home.

When she walked into the house, Jamaal was asleep in his room and Anthony was in their bed. Maria took a shower and got into the bed with him. She leaned over and kissed Anthony on his forehead. He did not budge. Maria turned over not before praying and asking the Lord what to do with her messy life.

Chapter 9

The clock almost scared me half to death when it blared in my ear. I hit the snooze button with out opening my eyes. Movement in the bed startled me. I opened my eyes and saw Maria attempting to get comfortable. I looked at the clock. It read six a.m. I didn't remember Maria coming in, so I wondered what time she did. I turned to get out of the bed and Maria moved, too.

"Good morning. How did everything go?" she said, wiping her eyes.

"With what?" I asked.

"With Jamaal last night," she replied.

"Fine. You act as if I can't take care of my child. Everything went fine. How was your night out?" I questioned.

"It was okay. We just chilled and talked," Maria said.

I got up and walked into the bathroom to prepare for work. I showered, shaved and dressed. On the way out I heard Maria say something.

"What did you say?" I asked from the door.

"I love you," she shouted from the bedroom.

"I love you, too," I replied.

I walked out and headed to work.

When I walked into the work, Baines was asleep at his desk. I placed my things quietly down on my desk. I crept beside Baines, bent down close to his ear and in my commander's best voice, I screamed, "I know you are not sleeping on my shift soldier."

Baines jumped up from the desk and stood straight up and yelled, "No, sir."

I fell to my knees in laughter. The look on his face was so funny I couldn't help but laugh.

"Man, you ain't funny," he said, sitting down.

"What's up with you? You had a rough night?" I teased.

"Yeah, man. For some reason the ole lady wanted to be real touchy feely. We had a long night," Barnes answered.

"See, I told you. You suppose to sleep at night and get it in the morning on nights you know you need sleep," I informed him.

"Man, I can't do that. I don't like getting up in the morning as is," Baines said.

"That's why you get it in the morning. That way busting one in the morning will get you going long enough to get you up and ready for work," I said, smiling.

"You think you know everything, don't you, man?" Baines joked.

"About the ladies…yeah, I do. I'm a Mac," I said, tugging at my shirt.

"Yeah, you like to eat Big Macs at MacDonald's. That's the only dealings, with macness you have," he said.

"You corny as hell." I laughed.

"Man, let's get out there and do some work before our asses be on PT and no one will be getting anything for a while," Baines said.

We worked and joked the rest of the day. I was so tired driving home, but all I could think about was the left overs from yesterday.

"That gurl did her damn thang," I said to myself.

That food was so good. I was getting hungry thinking about it. I pulled up to the complex and parked. I reached the door in no time. I opened the door and threw my bag on the floor. I headed straight to the kitchen, washed my hands and began taking the left over food out of the fridge. I cut on the television and plopped down on the sofa to enjoy my food. Halfway into the local news I realized how quiet the house was. I finished my pork chops and walked to the back of the apartment. I checked Jamaal's room and my room. I was home alone. I went back into the den to finish my food, but got thirsty afterwards. On the way to the trash can, I went to the kitchen to get a Corona when I saw the white piece of paper stuck to the top. I grabbed the paper and unfolded it to read.

Anthony,

I have had a lot of things on my mind lately. The more I try to love you, the more I feel you pushing me away. I don't understand and I am very confused. I know you are probably wondering why I am writing you instead of talking to you one on one but I feel better this way. I don't want to fuss with you and I don't want to cry no more. I love Jamaal and I love you, but I feel I need to get away, so that I can think about things and come to a conclusion about my life. Please don't look for me because only my mother will know where I am and she promised not to tell you. She will have Jamaal if or when you want to see him. I don't know when I will be back. Don't look for me. I will contact you daily to let you know I am okay. I hope you understand. I love you.

Maria

I looked at the letter front and back. I folded it back up and placed it back on the refrigerator. I sat down at the kitchen table in disbelief. Shaking my head continuously.

"What the hell?" was all I could manage to get out. I sat for a moment longer and then instantly jumped up. It was like a light bulb popped on in my head I got up and grabbed the phone.

"Mrs. Fields. How are you?" I asked.

"I'm okay, baby. How are you?" she asked with a hint of concern in her voice.

"I will be okay once I find out what is going on," I said.

"Yes, baby, I know. Everything is okay. And it will be okay. The baby is fine. Do you want to talk to him?" she asked.

"Yes, I would like that," I replied.

I heard Mrs. Fields yell for Jamaal to come to the phone.

"Daaddyy?" Jamaal called as if he was wondering if it was me.

"Yes, Lil Man, it's Daddy. How are you?" I asked.

He didn't respond.

"Jamaal?" I called.

"Yes?" he replied.

"Whatcha doing?" I asked.

"I play with Dada," Jamaal said.

"Okay, man. You keep playing with Dada," I said.

Jamaal handed Mrs. Fields the phone back. I heard him run back to where he came from.

"Anthony? You there?" Mrs. Fields asked.

"Yes, ma'am. I'm here. Do you know what's going on?" I asked.

"Well, baby, all I know is Maria came here crying about being confused. She didn't say about what. Then she had the baby and his clothes, asked me if I could keep him for a little while. But when I asked her what a little while was, she said she didn't know for sure. She dropped the Baby off, told me where she would be and that she'll be okay. She made me promise not to tell you where she was going. You not beatin' my daughter are you?" she asked.

"No, ma'am, I've never hit her. She's hit me a couple of times, but I've never laid a hand on her," I said.

"Good. Now it seems to me she's just a little stressed," Her mom said.

"How's that? She's never here. Every time I turn around she's there with your family," I protested.

"Uh? What do you mean, son? I haven't seen Maria since y'all came for Dada's birthday," her mom said.

By this time, I was really confused.

"But Ma Fields, that was a month ago. Ever since that weekend, Ri had been leaving the house with Jamaal for weekends at a time. Leaving on Fridays and coming back on Sunday nights. So if she won't there, where was she, with my child at that!?" I began to talk loudly.

"Now calm down, Chile. Something do sound strange, though. Listen, I got Jamaal. You try to relax for the rest of the week. Call as often as you like to check on the baby, but he's in good hands," she said.

"Yes, ma'am," I agreed.

I hung up the phone and stood in the middle of the floor. I did not know what to do. My head was spinning from all the chaos. I walked into the den and laid on the couch. I could not believe Maria left. Over and over again I thought about reasons why she would leave. We had an understanding. I thought. I closed my eyes to relax. I heard keys turning into the door. I sat up anxiously. Maria walked through the door but did not have Jamaal.

"Maria. Why did you just leave that way? And where's Jamaal?" I asked.

"I left him with my parents. We need to talk," she said.

She sat next to me on the couch and leaned over.

"What do we need to talk about? What's wrong with you?" I asked.

"You don't love me. You love Lisa. So why are we doing this?" she asked.

"Because that's what you wanted. I only wanted a baby and

you told me you'd give me one. You volunteered. And then you wanted to get married. You made yourself like this," I said to her.

"What do you mean? You said okay. You shouldn't have agreed to marry me. So you don't want me? You want a bitch dat don't want your ass!" She began to scream as tears rolled down her face.

I didn't understand why she was doing this. She knew from day one how I felt about Lisa. This wasn't a surprise to her, I looked at her and took a deep breath.

"Look. I told you from the jump about the feelings I had and have for Lisa. Hell, you knew. You saw how I talked to her all the time and how I acted when I was done, but you stuck around anyway, thinking you were gonna change me. You can't change me. Only I can change me! But yet you mad at me, like I tried to hide shit from you," I yelled.

"You are so stupid, why can't you see you need to move on? Why do you I have to suffer? I love you, why can't you love me, too?" she cried.

"I do love you, but not like you want me to. I can't I can't just by the way we got together. You knew how I felt about someone else but you still wanted to have a baby with me," I told her.

"Oh, so because I gave you what you wanted you can't love me?" she asked.

"I will always love you because you birthed my child, but I am not in love with you. And you will just have to take that as you want."

There was suddenly loud banging at the door. I jumped up to see who wanted to get in so bad. I tripped to the door and opened it. David was standing on the other side.

"What the hell is wrong wit you? What you doing in here?" David asked.

"I—I." I turned around to show David that Maria and I were talking but no one was on the couch. I rushed to the back, looked in all the rooms and bathrooms, but no one was there except me. I slowly walked back to the door to David looking at me like I was crazy. At that moment I felt crazy.

"What in tha hell?" David screamed.

He walked through the door and stood in between me and the television.

"Have you been smoking?" he asked with his arms folded across his chest.

"Naw man. See what happened was I came home and I was eating when I noticed RiRi and Maal won't here. Then I went to get a Corona and saw a note…"

David interrupted me.

"Please get to the point of why you are running around here acting like you crazy as hell," he yelled.

I took a deep breath and shortened my story.

"Well, Maria left and won't tell me where she is, Jamaal is with her mom. I thought she came back but obviously I was dreaming and you woke me up banging like the police," I said.

"You have lost your damn mind," David said, walking to the love seat to sit.

"No, let me finish," I said, preparing to tell my story.

David sat back in the seat and waited for me to begin.

"I came home and there was a note on the fridge. Hell. It still on the fridge. Anyway, I called her mom and she told me that she knows where Maria is but she can't tell me," I said, pausing.

"What do you mean she can't tell you? That's your wife. What kind of shit is that?" David yelled.

I interrupted him.

"Now, but get this. You know how every weekend Maria and Jamaal been going to D.C. to her parents?" I asked.

David shook his head in agreement.

"Well, Mrs. Fields said she hasn't seen then since we went up there a month ago for Maria's dad's birthday," I said, shaking my head.

"Damn, man, something sound real funny," David said.

"But what gets me is that my son has been out with her GOD only knows where," I said.

"Man, I am eager to see what all this is about. How long you think she'll be gone?" David asked.

"I don't now," I said.

"What you gonna do about Maal?" he asked.

"Well, I'm gonna let him stay, but I'm gonna go visit him the weekend. I don't want to bring him home alone because he gonna ask questions about Maria. See right now he probably think that he just visiting his grandparents." I shrugged my shoulders.

"Yeah, I guess you right," David agreed.

I laid back on the couch wondering what my next step would be. The room was silent for a while. David knew that I wasn't much for conversing but just his presence made me feel a whole lot better. David reached over to the coffee table and grabbed the remote control. He flipped through the channels for an hour and a half before he decided to speak again.

"You hungry?" he asked.

"Naw, I'm straight," I said.

David's phone rung and from the subject of the conversation, I knew it was Rita.

"Yeah. He's right. I don't now. You worrying me now. I'm gonna be here for a little bit. Let me go. Okay. Yeah me, too. Bye." David slammed his phone on the table.

I sat up and looked at him. "Man, if you need to go I understand," I said.

"Naw man, I'm okay. She'll be okay. She just worrisome as all out that's all. Don't want nothing but to worry me to death," he said. He walked into the kitchen and opened the fridge. "I'm gonna get one of those Coronas, man," David asked in only the way he could.

"Go head. I don't care," I said.

I heard David pop the top off the beer but he remained in the kitchen. I knew he was reading the letter that Maria left, but I did not care. He slowly walked back into the den and sat down.

"Some shit, ain't it?" I asked.

"Yeah, man, I ain't neva seen anything like it," he said.

"It's like some movie stuff," I said.

"Yeah, I know," David replied.

At that very moment I had a sudden urge to call Lisa. I sat up on the couch and glared at the television.

"What bright idea do you have now?" David asked.

I smiled because he always knew me. "What do you mean?" I asked.

"Nigga don't play me. You up to something," he said.

"Nothing, but I'm about to go for a ride. You gonna be here when I get back?" I asked.

"When you get back? I'm going to keep your black ass out of trouble," he said.

"Not an option," I replied.

"Where you going?" he asked.

"Not for you to know," I said.

"Man, well I'm gone. You call me when you stop acting like you on drugs," he said.

He finished his beef and tossed the bottle into the trash can. He gave me dap on the way out of the door.

"Call me when you get back to normal," he demanded.

"No problem," I said, closing the door.

As I prepared to ride out my cell phone rung.

"Hello?" I shouted.

"Damn boy why you so loud?" Kim asked.

"Heeeyyy, what's up, Kim?" I said.

I tried to sound as happy as I could. I needed to get Maria's messed up shit out my head.

"I got a party. You in?" she asked.

I stood at the kitchen counter and thought for a minute. Why shouldn't I go have some fun? I needed to get my mind off things and seeing Lisa may not have been a good thing.

"Hell yeah, I'm in. What's the detail?" I asked.

I took a piece of paper and a pen and jotted down the info.

"Cool, I'll be there in about an hour," I told Kim.

"You will be very satisfied. Oh, by the way, watch what you do," she whispered in the phone.

I quickly caught her code and replied, "Cool. Good looking gurl."

I hung up the phone and dashed to my bed room to take a military shower. I hopped in and back out in about three minutes. I put on my clothes, picked up my black bag and left the apartment. I arrived at the party site and called him.

"I'm here yo," I said to Kim.

"Come to the back of the joint and knock three times slow," she instructed.

"What kind of mess y'all running?" I laughed.

"Just come on," she demanded.

I got out the car and headed to the building. Before I could even knock, she opened the door.

"Hey, man. What's up?" she asked.

"Cooling. You got a place for me?" I asked.

"You know it," she responded.

I followed Kim to a room at the back of the building. I walked in and prepared for the party. A few moments later, Kim knocked on the door.

"Are you ready for your grand entrance Mr. Superstar?" Kim giggled.

"Just as sure," I told her.

I opened the door and walked out.

"Loooking good, sexy man," Kim commented.

"Thanks. How's the crowd?" I asked.

"Fair," she replied.

We stopped at the door.

"Wait for me to introduce you," she instructed.

I did as I was told. When she walked into the large room I heard yelling and screaming, glasses clanking and loud music. Suddenly a hush came over the crowd as Kim began to speak.

"Listen here I have a real special treat for y'all tonight. Some of you may have seen him before and for the rest of you, it may be your first time. Regardless, this brotha will bring you all to your knees. Without further interruption, I present to you VA's finest, Chocolate Seaman."

Kim flung the door open as the D.J. played "Imagine That" by R. Kelly.

I walked into the room dressed in all black leather. The women went wild. A unison of "Ah shit," was heard from the fellas. It was cool, though. I could imagine their surprise thinking they would have a nice evening out with their ladies and a fine brotha, not to mention stripper, comes bouncing in the spot. Kim had already had my props set up so I was good to. Woman rushed the stage as their men rushed the bar. To talk about me, I had no doubt, but it was cool with me. I'd be taking home their hard earn money. Half way through my performance a distinctive face caught my eye. I continued my routine as I tried to decipher where I had seen this woman. The lights were really low and between that and the mask I was wearing, it was hard to see. During the final song," Slow Wind" by Toni Tony Tone, I pulled apart my leather pants leaving me nothing but my black Navy boots and a black leather g-sting. The familiar woman's eyes almost popped out her head. At that very moment it all became clear. It was Lisa. "Thank GOD you have a mask on," I said in my mind. It was beginning to make sense why Kim told me to wear it. She must have known that had she told me there would be a possibility that Lisa would be there, I would not have come. I focused on Lisa as I poured hot candle wax on my body. She was in to it, I could tell by the look in her eyes. I danced to the part of the stage where she stood. I quickly grabbed her hand and placed it on my crotch. I pumped three times. The third time sent her hand flying above her head. All the woman screamed. Some shouting, "Do me!" Others were yelling, "Let me feel it, too." I went back to the middle of the stage for my exit. The lights went completely out and the crowd was silent. Suddenly a purple light fell on me as the D.J. played my exit song, the verse of Prince's "Nikky." As Prince sang, "Come back, Nikky, come back," for the final time, I moved my body against the floor before falling completely out and the room being pitch black. I hurried off the stage back to the disclosed room. I heard the women screaming and yelling. Three knocks at the door let me know Kim was at the other side. I opened the door and there she stood wit a huge Kool-Aid smile on her face.

"As I expected. You knocked them dead. I see you saw why I told you to wear your mask." She smiled.

"Why didn't you tell me?" I asked.

"Because I knew you wouldn't come." She smiled.

"And I know that's right." I smiled.

"Well, once again, Mr. Sea-Man," she patted me on my back.

"How did I let you talk me into this? My command would kill me if he knew I did this…And let's not get on Maria," I said.

"Yeah, lets not ruin your wonderful night," she said, handing me a box full of money.

"Thanks. I needed this boost," I said, taking the money and packing my things. "No problem. Let me know when you're ready to go and I'll make sure the coast is clear," Kim said.

She exited the room and I quickly changed. I text messaged Kim to inform her that I was ready and she guided me out to the car unseen. I threw my things into the trunk and got into the car.

"Mis-ter Sea-Man, uh?" Lisa said, smiling.

I grabbed my chest because she had scared the shit out of me.

"Gurl how you get in here? You scared the shet out of me!" I yelled.

She laughed. I took a deep breath and turned the ignition. The Quiet Storm was playing.

"How did you know it was me?" I asked.

"Don't you think I should now someone I fuck when I see him?" she asked.

"Oh we fuck? Ya man know?" I asked.

"Ya wife know?" she replied.

"Okay. You got me. But for real. How'd you guess?" I asked.

"Well, I didn't really know until the end. When 'Nikky' played and your ass pumped that floor. A chill came over me. I know it was you," she said.

"Really?" I asked.

"Yeah, not to mention that action you gave my hand. I know how you feel." She smiled.

"Your parents never told you not to sneak into cars unannounced. You can get shot doing that shet!" I said.

"I know. But I had to let you know what you did to me in there," Lisa said.

"What did I do?" I asked.

"I can show you betta than I can tell you!" she said.

Lisa grabbed my hand and placed them down her pants and panties. My fingers were completely soaked.

"Damn. You need to watch that." I smiled.

"Maybe you should watch it for me," she said.

She climbed over to me straddling my lap. She slowly began to kiss me as I looked around.

"What, you scared?" she teased.

"Just not trying to catch a charge. You know I'm in the military. They expect more of us!" I said.

"Well, they are not around, but I am. I want you," she said.

"What is all this about?" I asked.

"All what?" she asked.

"I mean you all over me and stuff. Didn't your man just sign a huge contract or something," I asked.

"Well he's not here and you danced to me. So you were just teasing me?" she asked. She knew how to get me.

"I'd never tease you," I said.

"Well, give it to me," she moaned.

"Damn. You horny," I said.

"Take care of it then," she said.

I slipped my hands under her shirt and caressed her breasts. We began to kiss. She unbuckled my pants and released my manhood. She pulled her pants down and sat on my lap. I gently cupped the back of her neck and head. I guided her along my manhood. The more she slid up and down the more I squeezed.

"Anthony. You feel so good," she groaned.

"Show me," I whispered.

Before I could tell her again she had climaxed all over me. She tightly gripped my manhood in her canal and I suddenly exploded also. We were both exhausted. She got up and wiped off as best as she could.

"Where did the towel come from?" I asked.

"I bought it with me," she answered.

"Did you set me up?" I smiled.

"Nope," she quickly answered.

We sat and conversed until the morning. I even had to move my car once people exited the building from the party.

My ride home was so peaceful I smiled the whole way. I felt relieved. Someone wanted not only me, but to spend time with me. For a long time I had not felt the way Lisa made me feel and I will remember it for a long time to come. Not because Lisa found out that I stripped on the side, because Kim probably told that a long time ago, but because for once in my life I wanted someone who wanted me, too.

Chapter 10

The week passed so quickly that Maria began to panic. She knew she had to make a decision about her life but she was not sure of what she would do. Maria walked through the penthouse suite in her pajamas contemplating her next move.

"What is wrong with you walking back and forth? You gonna wear a whole in the floor. And I'm not paying for that!" Devonna teased.

Maria stopped walking and sat down on the couch across from her secret lover.

"What is wrong with you?" Devonna asked once more.

"I'm so confused. A damn week has passed and I still haven't made a decision about anything," Maria whined.

"Don't worry about that. I got this room for as long as you need it. I told you that. I've been here with you since Wednesday and that may not necessarily be good for you. Because I may be clouding your judgment. So I want you to enjoy your weekend, but I'm leaving Sunday. The front desk has my card number, so you can leave what ever day you want," Devonna said.

Maria could not believe that Devonna was willing to go through so many changes to make her happy. She began to think about the time she had spent with Anthony. She wanted to see if he had taken the leaps that Devonna has for her. With all that she could remember, none of her memories consisted of Anthony doing all he could for her. The majority of their relationship was pretty much an agreement. She had his baby. He gave her money, clothes, jewelry but not much time. He always spent most of his time at work, away with work related jobs or out with his cousins. Maria looked over at Devonna watching television. She then began to think about what Devonna had to offer her. As she thought about what Devonna did for her, she smiled. She felt a certain level of happiness over come her body. Maria thought about how Devonna talked with her, gave her hugs when she needed them, never pressured her to have sex, listened to her and most of all spent time with her. Maria stretched out on the couch still smiling. Devonna looked over at her.

"What the hell is that crazy psycho smile for?" she asked.

Maria sat up to speak.

" I was just thinking about all the things you've done for me since we've known each other. You've not only been a lover but a friend to me," Maria said.

"Okay and for that you have a crazy smile?" Devona teased.

"Yes, because I don't have a friendship with Anthony. I mean we used to until I decided I would have Jamaal and then it became more like a contract agreement," Maria explained.

"Oh, okay," Devonna said.

Maria blew Devonna a kiss. Devonna motioned as if to catch the kiss and placed it on her forehead. Devonna turned around and continued to watch television. The two women watched television in silence for a half hour before Maria spoke.

"I've decided what I want to do," Maria blurted out.

"You excited ain't you?" Devonna teased.

"Yes. I am Heffa!" Maria said.

"Well?" Devonna asked.

"Well, I've decided that I'm gonna leave Anthony," Maria said.

Devonna slowly turned towards Maria. She was so surprised that she could not speak. In her mind, she never thought she'd see the day that Maria would leave Anthony.

"Are you going to respond?" asked Maria.

Devonna took a deep breath and spoke.

"Is that what you really want?" she asked.

"Yes, well, no. I mean I want to be happy and Anthony is not doing it," Maria said.

"You sound like you're not sure," Devonna said.

"I'm sure I want to be happy. It's just finding that happiness, that I'm not sure about," Maria explained.

"You first have to make sure you get rid of the things that make you unhappy first," Devonna said.

"I know. Anthony doesn't make me absolutely unhappy, but he doesn't make me happy either," Maria said.

Maria laid back down on the couch and watched television. Devonna looked at her. Maria seemed to be lost. It hurt Devonna so bad that she could not help her, but she knew Maria had to make the decision on her own. It was her life and her decision.

Maria sat up on the couch and looked at her watch.

"Damn I fell asleep for two hours!" she said in disbelief. She looked around the room but did not see Devonna. She got up and walked into the kitchen. There was still no sign of her. Maria decided to walk to the bathroom to freshen up. When she reached the entrance of the bathroom she smelt candles burning. Maria walked to the doorway and stopped. Devonna was in the tub. It was full of bubbles, candles were burning all around the tub and she was drinking a glass of wine.

"Looking for me?" she asked.

"Nope. Not for real. Needed to used the bathroom," Maria answered nonchalantly.

"You're a liar. Undress," Devonna demanded.

"What!?" Maria gasped.

"Strip!" Devonna screamed playfully.

Maria complied to Devonna's orders excitedly.

She stepped into the tub and was caught off guard by the steaming hot water.

"Damn I know the bottom of your ass is melted like a bitch," she said.

"Stop crying and get in. It ain't hot," Devonna said, smiling.

Maria cautiously sat down and slowly began to relax.

"Your wine is right there," Devonna said, pointing behind Maria to the wine glass half full of red wine.

"You trying to get me drunk?" Maria asked.

"Only if you want to be," Devonna said, smiling.

Maria took the glass and drunk all of the wine in one take.

"Damn Baby, you need to slow that down," Devonnna said.

"With the week I've had, you betta be glad I didn't drink the whole bottle," Maria said.

Maria placed the empty glass on the floor behind the tub and moved closer to Devonna.

"What are you up to?" Devonna asked.

"Nothing," Maria replied, still moving.

Maria ending up being so close to Devonna that they were practically lip to lip. Devonna stroked Maria's hair as she passionately kissed her. They began to caress and fondle each other.

"Um. You feel so good," Devonna said.

"Show me how good I feel," Maria begged.

Devonna disappeared into the bubble filled tub. Maria felt Devonna between her legs. Devonna began to kiss and such on her thighs. She then moved over to her mound. The feeling was so intense that Maria's head fell back and hit the back of the tub. Devonna was pleasing Maria so well that she did not have time to figure out if her head hurt or not. Maria closed her eyes to enjoy the moment, but all she could think about was comparing Anthony's sexual pleasure to Devonna. She battled back and forth in her head on who's oral sex was the best. Suddenly Devonna hit Maria's G-Spot. She almost lost control. Maria began to scream and grab on Devonna's head as she climaxed. Maria pushed on Devonna's head So much that Devonna panicked, thinking she was going to drown. Devonna fought her way from in between Devonna's legs in just enough time to catch her breath. Devonna shot up from out of the water gasping for air.

"Gurl, are you trying to kill me!" Devonna huffed.

"I'm sooo sooorry," Maria said.

Maria grabbed Devonna, washed her face off and kissed her soft thick lips.

"Baby. I'm sorry but you know what you do to me," Maria apologized once again.

"It's okay. I know I be doing my thang," Devonna said, licking her lips.

They both looked at each other and burst into uncontrollable laughter. The women finished their baths and dried each other off. Maria was beginning to put on a clean pair of pajamas when Devonna stopped her.

"What are you doing? Put some clothes on, were going out to dinner," Devonna instructed.

Maria pulled out a pair of jeans, a blouse and her stiletto sandals.

"Why you trying to get hurt?" Devonna asked.

"What are you talking about?" Maria asked.

"You know people gonna be all over you with that on," Devonna said to Maria.

Maria smiled and walked to the door.

"You coming?" Maria asked with a smile.

"How you gonna ask me? You don't know your way around Maryland," Devonna said.

"I'm from D.C. I'll find my way," Maria replied.

"Okay, Miss Find My Way," Devonna said, joining Maria at the door.

Maria woke up, took a shower and dressed. She quietly packed her bags and tapped Devonna on the shoulder.

"Hey you. I'm gonna go back. I miss Jamaal and I know he misses me and his dad," Maria whispered to Devonna.

"You'll call me later?" Devonna asked.

"Yes, sweetie, I promise. Thank you for everything. Where will you be when you leave? D.C. or V.A.?" Maria asked.

"I don't know yet. I'll text you," Devonna said.

"Okay," Maria replied.

Maria walked out of the hotel and got into her car. The drive from Maryland to D.C. was a long and tiring one. Maria thought about her decision to leave Anthony and how she was going to do it. Darkness began to fall as Maria arrived to her parent's home. She took out her keys and unlocked the door.

"Hello!?" Maria yelled.

"Moommmyy," Jamaal yelled, running from the kitchen.

"Hey, baby. I missed you soo much. Mommy, sorry she left you. She won't ever do that again," Maria said, hugging and kissing her son.

"Ump. You decide to come home from running away? Where the hell you been? You had everyone worried sick about you. Especially your husband. You remember him…Anthony. The one who puts you in those expensive clothes and that too expensive car!" Maria's father screamed.

"Earl, leave the girl alone. She just walked in the house," Maria's mom walked into the hallway.

"Thanks, Mom," Maria said, rolling her eyes at her father and entering the kitchen.

"Do you have yourself together?" her mother asked, following her.

"Yeah, Ma, I'm together. I made some decisions about my life and I was wondering if Jamaal and I can move in with y'all," Maria said.

Maria's mother sat at the kitchen table with her. She folded her arms and looked deep into her face.

"What are you saying baby?" her mother asked.

"I'm saying. I'm leaving Anthony. I am not happy and...."

Maria's mother interrupted her, "Baby, you don't have to explain anything to me. If you're leaving you're leaving. That's all to it."

"Thanks, Mom. What about Dad? What will he say?" Maria asked.

"Don't worry about that. I will handle your father," her mother said, winking at her.

"Well, I'm gonna take Jamaal and we're gonna go home to pack the rest of our things and do that Anthony can see Jamaal," Maria said.

"You're sure that's a wise idea to take Jamaal with you?" her mother asked.

"Well, be okay, Mom," Maria assured her mother.

Maria headed to the door and called for Jamaal. They walked out of the door and headed for their home in Virginia.

When Maria and Jamaal arrived home it was eleven thirty at night and she had to tote him to the door. Maria opened the door, dropped Jamaal's bag at the door and kicked the door close. The door slamming frightened Anthony. He jumped up and ran towards the front of the apartment. He was shocked to see Maria standing there with Jamaal in her arms knocked out. He quickly rushed over to then and took Jamaal out of her arms.

"What's up with you?" he asked.

"Nothing much," Maria lied.

Anthony stood there for a moment wondering how she could stand there and say nothings wrong with her when she had just picked up and left with their child for a week. He didn't want to run her away again so he decided to hold off until tomorrow with the questions.

"I'm gonna put lil' man in the bed. You need anything?" Anthony asked.

"No. I'm just tired. I'm gonna take a shower and go to bed," Maria replied.

"Cool," Anthony said.

They both walked towards the back of the apartment going they're different ways. Anthony pulled off his son's clothes and put his pajamas on without walking him. He placed him in the bed and pulled the covers on top of him. He knelt down at Jamaal's bed and prayed.

"Lord I thank you for bringing my
son home safely. You are the only
one who truly knows why his moms
left with him. I know our marriage
may not be like she wants it to be
but I can't hide what's in my
heart. And being that you know and
see all, what's the point of me
faking? I don't know why she
choose to say yes to having my
child. I will always love her
because of that Lord. And anything
I can do for her and Jamaal I will
But I can't fake it anymore. Lord
I just thank you for letting both
Them be okay and coming home okay.
Lord if this mess is my fault, I
Ask that you help me make it right
Amen.

Maria was standing at the door with tears stinging her face. She had no idea why she was crying but she knew she had made the right decision to leave. Hearing Anthony's prayer placed her in a prospective that she thought she'd never have to be in. She thought he could grow to love her. She tiptoed back into the room and climbed into the bed.

Anthony kissed his son on the forehead and returned to his own bed, not knowing what Maria had heard. He cupped her body and she began to cry, Anthony did not know his wife cried. Anthony did say a word. He just held her tight, kissed the back of her neck and prayed that she'd stop.

Both Anthony and Maria slept throughout the night. When Maria had awaken, Anthony still had a tight grip on her body. She did not know what to say. So she decided to start the day on a good note. She turned to face Anthony.

"Good morning. Have a bad dream?" she asked with a smile.

"Bad dream? No! Why you ask that?" Anthony responded, confused.

"I mean you holding me like the Boogie Man was out to get you!" she smiled.

"You funny," Anthony said, slowly releasing his grip.

"I'm just joking," Maria said.

She looked at Anthony and began to speak.

"Hey. I'm sorry," Maria slowly said.

"No apologies needed. I'm cool," Anthony said.

Maria looked over Anthony's shoulder at the clock.

"You not going to work?" she asked.

"Naw, I'm gonna chill today. Is there a problem with that? If so I can go ahead and go in," Anthony teased.

He moved as if he was going to get out of the bed. Maria pulled him back.

"No. I'd like for you to say," she said.

"Uh oh, you want me to stay home? What you plotting on?" he asked.

"Nothing. We do need to talk though. When ever you get a free moment," Maria said.

She took a deep sigh. It took all she had to muster up that statement. She knew that when ever she told Anthony that before he would leave the house and return when he knew she would be asleep. She looked at him. He had a complex look on his face. He matched her sigh before he spoke.

"Shoot. I got time now," he said, turning on his back. The statement caught Maria off guard she began to stutter.

"Well...I—I, um."

She laid on his chest and thought about her words.

"Anthony? I know we don't have the traditional marriage. I understand that. I know sometimes you wish you were with someone else."

Anthony opened his mouth to speak but Maria placed her two fingers on his lips.

"Let me finish. It took me a lot to gather my thoughts and I need to do this. I need to speak my mind," Maria said.

"Okay," Anthony replied.

Silence filled the room while Maria gained her strength to speak once more.

"You don't have to tell me if I'm right or wrong. It doesn't matter. I was wrong. Not only to you, but to myself for thinking I could change you and make you love me. I was even more wrong for thinking you'd love me more than you love her. You can't help who you love and I knew you loved her from the start, nut I just wanted somebody to love me like that. But I wasn't smart enough to realize that if you loved her like that, you couldn't possibly have room to love me like that, too. I'm just sad for you though. Because all this time I'm trying to get you to love me. You're in the same situation. You tying to get her to love you and she with somebody else. Maybe one day you'll figure it out. Well, I hope you do," Maria said.

She felt a burst of confidence. She sat up and sat on the edge of the bed. She looked out of the door straight into Jamaal's room and saw that he was still asleep. She turned around to see the shock on Anthony's face. His hands were folded behind his head, but he was still laying on his back. She thought he was going to respond to what she had said so far, but he didn't. She decided to continue.

"Look. What I am trying to say is that, um...I am leaving." She paused, still no response. In fact, he had not even moved.

"I mean what's the use of us being together if you don't love me? I just need to leave and wait for someone who will love me and take care of me. I'm not saying that you don't take care of me and Maal, but I just want someone to love me like I should be and if it won't be you, it might as well be room for somebody to." Maria stopped once more. She looked at Anthony. This time his eyes were closed.

"Anthony, I know you ain't sleep. Anthony!" Maria screamed.

She climbed over to him on the bed but could not get a response from him. She shook him very hard. She began to scream and cry.

"An-tho-ny. Ple-a-se listen. Please wake up!" she panicked. She grabbed the phone on the side.

"911 What's your emergency?" the operator answered.

"My husband. He not breathing or moving. Please help me," Maria screamed.

The screaming woke Jamaal. He came into the room, crying.

"Mommy?" Jamaal said.

"Go Mal. Go back in your room! Go lay down!" she screamed at him.

"Ma'am, calm down. Tell me what the problem is," the operator asked.

"I don't know. I was talking to him and then I noticed he won't moving,"

Maria screamed through the phone.

"Okay, ma'am, I'll try my best to help you until someone gets there," the operator assured Maria.

"Please. Oh my GOD. Please help," Jamaal ran into the bedroom and yelled. "Mommy, the abmbalamce is outside."

Maria dropped the phone and ran to the front door. The emergency workers ran passed Maria toward Jamaal who was in the doorway yelling.

"Here, Here. Get my daddy."

Maria sat down on the couch shaking not knowing what to do or how to think.

The emergency workers walked back and forth through the

apartment until she saw two men carrying Anthony out of the apartment on a gurney and into the emergency vehicle.

"What's going on? What's the matter with him? Where are you taking him?" Maria screamed.

A female worker went over to Maria, took her hand and motioned for her to have a seat. Maria complied. The worker waited for Maria to calm down before she spoke.

"Mrs. Lee, I need you to listen to me carefully. Are you calm enough to do that?" the worker asked.

Maria shook her head in affirmation.

"Okay. Your husband went into cardiovascular shock."

She paused to give Maria opportunity to speak.

"You mean he had a heart attack?" Maria asked.

"Yes, you can say that. We don't now why and that is why we have to take him to the hospital because we have to find out what exactly caused his heart to stop beating," the worker informed Maria.

Maria could not speak but continued to nod her head in agreement to show that she understood.

"Mrs. Lee, do you have someone you can call to bring you to the hospital?" she asked.

"Yes. I can call someone," Maria answered.

"Good we will take Mr. Lee to City General, all you have to tell them is who you are, who your husband is and they'll take it from there." The worker got up to exit the apartment. Maria followed her to the door. She extended her hand to the worker.

"Thank you so much," Maria said.

"No problem ma'am this is my job. Remember you're gonna want to get the hospital ASAP," the worker warned.

"I will. Thank you," Maria said, closing the door.

Maria sat down on the couch to attempt to regroup. As soon as she laid her head back on the edge of the table, she remembered her son.

"OH MY GOD. JAM-AAL!" Maria screamed running around the apartment looking for her son.

Maria walked in and out of the rooms but she could not find Jamaal. She stood in the middle of his room and began to cry. She fell to the floor and sobbed loudly. She heard a creek from Jamaal's closet door. She turned quickly to see Jamaal creep from his closet.

"Oh my goodness, baby. Are you okay?" Maria asked.

Jamaal shook his head and sat on his mother's lap.

"Mommy. I want my daddy," Jamaal cried.

"I know, baby. It will be okay. Everything scared you. Even Mommy. She is sorry for yelling at you, baby. You forgive Mommy?" Maria asked.

"It's okay, Mommy," Jamaal said, stroking his mother's long black hair. Maria did not know what to do but cry. She knew Jamaal stroking her hair let her know that things will be okay. Maria took ten minutes to bond with her son then she got up to call David.

"What nigga. What?" David answered.

"Um, David?" Maria spoke softly.

"My bad, Ri. What's up?" he asked.

"I need a favor. Can you get Daniel to keep Jamaal and you take me to the hospital?" she asked.

"Why? What's wrong with you and where is damn Anthony?" David asked.

"In the hospital, he had a heart attack. The ambulance had to take him to the hospital," Maria sniffed.

"Heart attack? What the fuck? Me and Rita on the way," David shouted and hung up the phone.

Maria went into the bedroom and threw on some clothes. She washed her face as well as Jamaal's and placed him on a jogging suite and sneakers. Just as she was tying his shoe laces David was banging on the door. Maria opened the door to Rita's questions.

"Oh my GOD gurl. What happened? You tried to kill him? Where he at? Where were y'all? Was y'all do-ing—"

David interrupted her.

"Rita. SHUT DA HELL UP! The girl's husband is in the hospital. Shut your pie hole and just let the woman get her thoughts together," David screamed.

Maria managed to crack a small smile. Not because she was happy, but because she was relieved that David made Rita hush up.

"This is the plan. We gonna take Rita and Maal to the crib. I don't know why she had to come in the first place. Anyway, then we will go check on Ant. Danny is on his way to CG now," David instructed.

"That sounds good," Maria said.

They all walked out of the apartment to the care. David dropped Rita and Jamaal off at his apartment.

"And don't call me. I'll call you," David yelled to Rita.

"Ok-ay nigga. Damn," she yelled back.

David sped off.

"Thank you so much David. I don't know what's going on. We were in bed. I told him I was leaving and he didn't move," Maria cried.

"Damn," David said.

He did not know if his cousin had the heart attack before his wife told him she was leaving or after. The remainder of the ride to the hospital was in complete silence. As both David and Maria thought about what kind of condition Anthony would be in when they arrived.

Chapter 11

I woke up with mad people around me and Maria with her finger underneath my nose.

"Gurl, what is wrong with you?" I yelled, pushing her hand away from my face.

"Anthony you had me worried sick," she said, hugging me.

I attempted to get up from the bed but my body felt like a ton of bricks.

"Naw man don't get up. What you need?" my cousin David asked, getting up from the chair in the corner of the room.

"Man, what the fuck is going on?" I asked him.

"You want me to tell you now or later, when your company leaves?" David asked I looked around the room to see who was actually in the room. I saw Maria, Kim, Daniel and my co-worker Baines. I looked and signaled for him to bend down close to my mouth.

"Look I want to talk now and I don't want company right now. Can you let everyone know I appreciate them coming down but I want to be alone," I whispered to him.

David took a deep sigh and collected his thoughts together. He cleared his voice and spoke. "Um, y'all!? Anthony would like to be alone for a little while, as he is being informed of his situation. He told to make sure I tell y'all that he appreciates you visiting and that you are welcomed back tomorrow during visiting hours," David announced.

My visitors began dispersing from the room but Daniel and Maria stayed. She walked over to me and sat on the side of the bed.

"You tired, baby?" she asked me.

I didn't feel strong enough to talk loud but I know she could hear me.

"Ri-Ri. I want to be with David and Daniel alone."

"Excuse me?" she asked.

She stood up and began to be herself. "I am your wife. I know you ain't 'bout to."

Daniel interrupted her. "Look, Maria. He needs time to himself. He has been through some shit right now."

I was glad he said something instead of me cursing her out. For all I know she had something to do with all of this.

Maria looked at me and I looked away. She then looked David and Daniel sucked her teeth and stormed out of the room.

"Damn, you got something on your hands man," David teased.

"She'll get over it," I replied.

The room became intensely quiet. I looked over at Daniel. He was staring out of the window. I then looked at David. He appeared to be playing a game on his cell phone.

"Can y'all niggas stop avoiding what I need and want to know?" I slowly said.

David looked up.

"What? That you a broke down pimp with one chick losing it and trying to kill you and the other about to marry somebody else?" David joked.

"Nigga you sick!" I said.

"I'm sick? You got it twisted dog. I'm here to see you," David teased.

Daniel walked over to my bed and sat on the edge of it.

"Okay. I'll tell you what's going on," he said.

"Here we go. Mr. ER in here. Like you a doctor," David teased.

"Okay. Tell me something. Somebody," I shouted.

Just as Daniel began to speak someone walked in.

"Ah, Mr. Lee, you're awake. How are you? My name is Dr. Kruns and I'll be attending to you during your stay."

I nodded my head in agreement to ensure the doctor that I understood. He continued to speak.

"Now. I see you had some complications uh? Well let me tell you, you are not the first young man to have a heart attack. And trust me, you certainly won't be the last," the doctor said, looking at his chart and looking back at me.

"How could this happen, doc? I am in good health. I work out and I eat well," I pleaded.

"Well, Mr. Lee, some things we can't explain and your case is one of them. My colleagues and I have gone over your tests and charts many times. We do see that you've had a heart attack but we can not pen point exactly what caused it," the doctor said, dropping his arms down to his side.

"Well, how long will I be here?" I asked.

"I'm looking to have you out of here in three days," he said.

"Three days?" I exclaimed.

"Yes, we need to keep an eye on you and continue to run some tests. You'll be fine. I'll make sure the finest nurse come by to take care of you," the doctor joked, giving me a wink.

"That's what's up doc, can I get a bed rolled in for me? My cuz can't bear all the excitement alone," David joked.

The doctor laughed as he walked out of the room.

I looked at David. He was looking at me with concern.

"What the hell is that look for?" I asked.

"No reason. You alright, man?" he asked.

"I'm cool. Just shocked by the whole situation," I said, deeply sighing.

"I know. This shit is wild," David said. Daniel got up from his chair and walked over to the bed.

"Ant man, tell me what happened with you and your girl," he said.

"Man. All I know is she ran off with Jamaal. Then she showed back up talking about leaving for good," I said, attempting to sit up in the bed.

"You need help?" David asked.

"Naw. I'm cool. But anyway. I knew this was gonna happen. I mean she and I had a lot of stuff different from one another," I continued.

I pushed myself all the way up on the bed, as I attempted to finish my story.

"I listened to her talk. I was gonna tell what ever she wanted to do we could. I just want to see Jamaal whenever I can and want to," I said.

"But did you know when your heart attack began?" Daniel asked.

"I don't know. She was talking and I felt a sharp pain in my arm, but I just laid there, hoping that it would go away. One minute I heard her voice and the next it was dead as silence," I explained.

"Damn man, I can't even imagine the feeling," David said.

"Naw you can't imagine Rita saying she'll leave yo ass, that's what you can't imagine," Daniel teased.

"Sometimes I wish she'd carry her ass." David laughed.

I laid there for a while in silence still wondering why it had to happen to me. Daniel and David was still joking when a huge flower arrangement walked through the door.

"Damn, has the rumor gone around that you dead already?" David asked as he burst into laughter.

"No, smart ass, I think that they're actually cute," the female voice behind the flowers said as she was placing them by her side.

"Lisa, what's up?" I asked, surprised to see Lisa standing in the doorway of my hospital room.

"Nothing, trying to see what is up with you!" she said.

Lisa handed the bouquet of flowers to David and pointed at the table beside my bed.

"What the hell does that mean? I ain't no dog. And I ain't deaf either. I speak English," David teased.

"Well, in that case, put the flowers on the desk and beat feet!" Lisa said with a huge smile.

"Oh, like that?" David asked.

He turned and looked at me.

"Well, I guess it's like that man," I said.

"That's foul. C'mon Daniel take me to the crib. I'll see this sap ass nigga later," David said, trying to sound as pitiful as he could.

"Aight. Look man, I'll see you later and nice to see you again Lisa," Daniel said, walking out behind David.

"Yeah bubble head. Nice seeing you!" David teased Lisa.

"You too. Now let me see the back of your head get small!" Lisa laughed.

The two walked out of the door and left Lisa and I alone.

"So who do I owe this pleasant surprise to?" I asked.

"None other than Kimberly." She smiled.

I patted the bed, indicating that she should have a seat. She sat down next to me. I attempted to hug her. She leaned back to meet me.

"You feel good," I whispered in her ear.

"Do I? Why?" she replied.

"You do. I'm glad you're here," I said.

"Why are you here with only your cousins? Where's your wife?" she asked.

I took a deep sigh and answered.

"Your guess is just as good as mine," I answered.

She gave me a crazy look and turned on the television.

"So exactly what is wrong with you?" she asked.

"Oh, you mean Kim didn't tell that part?" I asked.

"Naw, she just told me that it was a heart complication," she said.

"Yeah, they said I had a heart attack. I gotta stay here for three days," I informed her.

We sat back and watched television for a while. She turned to me and stared me straight in the eyes.

"What happened to us?" she asked.

The question caught me off guard so for a minute I just stared back and blinked. I can imagine how I looked. Like those chicks who trying to get into a club, but they're under age so they're in total shock when the bouncer says that they can't get in. I took a deep breath and slowly began to speak.

"I messed up," I confessed.

"Look don't worry about that, especially not now. You need to rest," she said to me, rubbing my legs.

"So how's your big time athlete?" I asked.

"Rodney? He's okay. A tad busy. But okay," she replied.

"Oh, so does this mean y'all gonna be moving the date of your wedding up?" I asked.

"You know something I don't know?" she replied.

I looked at her really funny. She must have received my signal because she shifted on the bed and then spoke again.

"We never sat a specific date. He asked, I said yes, and that was it," she replied.

I looked at her and then back at the television. There was silence for a moment.

"Maria and I are getting a divorce," I announced.

She sat up and looked dazed from the news. "What do you mean? I am so sorry," she said.

"No need to be. It's probably best."

"Who asked for what?"

"Well, I thought about it a lot. Just didn't know how to go by it without making her mad and taking a chance of not seeing Jamaal every day."

"So she asked? I never would have thought that would happen."

"Well, more like she told me. She left for a few days, I guess to get her mind together and then she came home, laid in the bed with me, began to talk about it and then I woke up here."

"Oh my GOD. You had your heart attack when your wife told you she wanted a divorce?"

"Yeah, something like that. I don't think it was the news that did it, though."

"I hope it wasn't."

"Well, I'll just be glad when I can get out of here," I finally said, taking a deep breath and closing my eyes. I felt Lisa looking at me, but I kept my eyes closed.

"You look tired. Probably from all the visits and doctors poking at you and stuff. Maybe I should go," she said.

"No. I'm enjoying your company. Please stay. If you don't mind," I said.

She looked at me and gently stroked my face.

"If you want me to stay, I will for a little while," she said.

"Will that interfere with any plans with your man?" I asked.

"No he's practicing for the first game," she said.

"Oh, so they don't get to go home?" I asked.

"No, they have like a huge dorm and all they all stay there. Funny, uh? He really didn't like staying on campus at school but he has to stay in a dorm for the first few weeks of the season." She laughed.

"Damn, what they breaking them in or something?" I asked.

"I guess it's because he's so young and hasn't graduated they want to make sure he has a good head on his shoulders and won't act the fool because he's making so much money," she said.

"Oh, well whatever," I responded.

"What time is it?" Lisa asked.

"You don't see that huge clock over there?" I teased.

"Oh yeah, okay. Damn it's nine already. I've been here three hours?" she said, surprised at the time. She flipped through the television stations. I dozed off and on, the next thing I remembered was waking up and seeing Lisa asleep beside me peacefully. I looked at the clock on the wall. It read 3:00 a.m.

"Damn," I said underneath my breath.

"Um?" Lisa groaned.

"Lisa. It's late. Do you have to go to work?" I asked her.

"Uh? What?" she moaned.

Lisa finally became conscious and sat up. She looked around. Then at me and then at the clock.

"OH SHIT! It's three in the morning?" she said.

"Yeah. I'm sorry we both fell asleep," I said.

"No problem, but I should be going so you can rest," she said.

"Only if you want to. I'm not kicking you out!" I replied.

"You tell me. I want to make sure you're okay. If you want me to stay I will, just say the word."

"The word," I teased.

"Fine, I hope you are comfortable because I refuse to sleep on anybody's chair!" she demanded.

I shifted so that I could make myself comfortable. It actually surprised me how big the bed actually was. She and I were both able to fit in the bed with no problem. Lisa got comfortable on top of the bed. She grabbed the extra blanket folded at the foot of the bed and wrapped up in it. She leaned over and kissed me on my cheek.

"Try to get some sleep, okay?" she said, settling back down on the bed.

I smiled to myself and laid back and got comfortable myself. We both rested, watching old sitcoms on television until we fell asleep.

The night nurse walked into the room to check Anthony's vitals.

"Ah, isn't that cute?" she said to herself as she changed

Anthony's fluid bags dripping into his IV. She quietly turned off the television after checking his vitals on the monitor. The nurse glanced at her watch to record the time for her records.

"Man, the night went by fast. It's six a.m.," she said under her breath.

She gathered her things and hustled out the room. She reached the door and turned to get once last glance of the adorable couple laying in the bed. She smiled once more, turned off the light and proceeded to the office to complete her shift. She walked out of the room to the nurse's station, where the other night nurses were gathering.

"You see the couple in room 308?" the nurse asked her co-worker.

"No, what about them? They are both hurt and in a room together?" her co-worker asked.

"No, the young man had a heart attack and she has been here since last night. They're both asleep on the bed. It's just too cute," the nurse exclaimed.

"Really? Let me see," the co-worker said, smiling.

The nurse walked down to Anthony's room and peeked through the window. Anthony was laying on his back inside of the bed and Lisa was on her side, facing Anthony wrapped in the extra blanket. The nurse smiled and returned to the station.

"You're right. They are too cute. It's nice to see young black couples sticking together like that," the second nurse said.

The morning shift were beginning to pile into the station to receive the shift updates. Anthony's nurse began speaking to the oncoming nurse about the patients.

"Oh yeah, the young man in 308 is adorable and so is his wife. I just checked his vitals and changed his fluid bags. He's all set until about ten when he'll need his vitals checked again," she stated.

The morning nurse looked at the night nurse with a frown on her face.

"That woman is back and was here all night?" she asked.

The night nurse then gave a look of her own.

"Yeah, they're asleep now. You had problems with them yesterday?" she asked.

"Well, the wife was leaving as I was and she cursed and yelled about how no one can kick her out of her husbands room and all this," the day nurse explained.

"Dang, you wouldn't think any of that by just looking at them last night, their interactions and them even now, as they sleep," the night nurse said.

"Ump," sighed the day nurse.

"Check for yourself," the night nurse urged.

The day nurse walked down to Anthony's room and returned quickly after.

"What is wrong with you? Why do you have that look on your face?" the night nurse asked.

"That is not his wife!" the day nurse exclaimed.

The night nurse was more confused than ever now.

The day nurse began to collect her things to begin her rounds when she turned and say Maria stepping off the elevator.

"Oh, shit. That's his wife," she said.

"I'm out. Fill me in later. I'm too tired for Jerry Springer today," the night nurse said, fleeing the station.

Chapter 12

The nurse tried to make herself look busy but Maria stepped up to the station and stopped.

"Good morning?" Maria strongly greeted the nurse to get her attention.

The nurse greeted Maria with her best smile.

"Um, yes. I just wanted to see how my husband was doing before I went to see him," Maria stated.

The nurse looked up and questioned.

"And which one is your husband?"

"Anthony Lee," Maria stated proudly.

The nurse look down her clipboard.

"Room 308, okay. Well, I just clocked in so I haven't done my rounds," the nurse stated without looking.

"Oh, okay. Have a nice day," Maria said and headed down the hall.

The nurse watched Maria walked down the hall and waited for a commotion to break out of the room.

Maria opened the door to Anthony's room.

"Good morning, baby," she exclaimed as she walked in.

Anthony took a deep breath and question his wife being there.

"What's up?" he asked.

"What's up? You not happy to see me?" she asked.

"I mean, for what?" he asked.

Maria ignored Anthony's question and sat in the chair close to the window. Just as she sat down to talk to Anthony she heard the toilet flush. Maria looked at Anthony. He looked back and rolled his eyes and looked at the television. Lisa walked out of the bathroom.

"Ant. You hun—gry?" she stuttered as she made eye contact with Maria.

"Oh is this why you questioned why I was here?" Maria sternly stated.

Lisa had never formally met Maria, but with the statement, she knew who she was. Anthony sat up in the bed and introduced his wife to his true love.

"Lisa, this is my wife...still wife, right?" he said, taunting Maria.

Maria rolled her eyes, Anthony continued.

"Maria-Lisa, Lisa-Maria," he quickly said and looked at Lisa.

Lisa was still in a bit of shock but she snapped out of it when Anthony began patting the bed, indicating that he wanted her to reclaim the spot she previously had.

"Anthony, Maybe I should go so that you and your wife can spend time with one another," Lisa said.

"You sure? It's up to you. No one's kicking you out," he insisted.

"No, I haven't been home. And that little wash up really didn't do it for me. Just call me if you need me okay?" Lisa said.

"Okay, maybe you need some real sleep. You had to have been cramped on this bed with me all night," Anthony replied.

Lisa looked at him and smiled. Her *Boy, you're a trip* smile.

Anthony smiled back as if to say, *I know*. Lisa walked over to Maria and extended her hand.

"Nice to finally get to meet you. Sorry it had to be under these circumstances."

"Damn, I'm not dead," Anthony teased.

Maria reluctantly shook Lisa's hand and put on her fakest smile.

"Yeah. I know. Thank you for keeping Anthony company. I really don't like hospitals," Maria said.

Anthony looked at Maria knowing that she could explode in a minute, he waited for it to happen.

"No problem. Anthony will always be a dear friend," Lisa said, shaking Maria's hand.

Lisa walked towards the door, stopped and turned around.

"Y'all have a good day. Get better, Anthony," she said.

Lisa walked out of the room and closed the door. As soon as she had, Maria's top completely blew.

"She stayed all night? You were fucking on your sick bed!" she yelled.

On the outside of the door Lisa heard the screaming as she walked towards the elevators. As she passed the nurse's station the nurse asked, "Is everything okay?"

Lisa slowed, "With me, yes. You may want to check on them though," she calmly stated boarding the elevator. Lisa headed home not thinking twice about he incident in the hospital.

"He'll be okay. He's a big boy. If he needs me, he'll call," she said to herself as she drove away form the hospital heading home.

Meanwhile, in Anthony's room, Maria was letting him have a piece of her mind.

"I can't believe you. You bastard! Here I am worried about your black ass, and you up here screwing that hooker." Maria paused. She looked at Anthony and waited for a response. He had none. He continued to look at the television.

"I know you hear me nigga. You not gonna say shit?" she asked.

He took a deep breath and finally spoke.

"Why you doing all of this? It's not because you're concerned for me. It's only because you're jealous. And why? You the one who wanted a divorce. Remember? Remember you the one who wants to leave and wait for someone to love and take care of you! Ain't that what you told me? So what's the big damn deal? And for your damn information, we did not have sex at all. Trust, though if she would have wanted to, I would have tore her ass up in here!" Anthony said.

Maria could not believe he had said that to her. She sat there with her mouth wide open.

"And close your damn mouth. Don't try to act shocked! It's my turn now. You said all that shit the other day thinking I wouldn't remember because of all the events that took place but I am not deaf. Not at all. I mean don't get it twisted. Nothings changed you want to leave and please don't let me stop you!" Anthony said.

He took a deep breath and felt relieved. Maria looked at him and stood up.

"Don't you at least want me to stay here while you're sleep?" she asked.

"Naw do whatever it is that you were gonna do today if I won't here. Today's Tuesday right?" he asked.

"Yes," she replied.

"So if I won't sick, you'd be gone by now right? So why don't you go home and get packed," he said.

She walked towards the door and stopped.

"I did already. I'll have David bring Jamaal over to see you. We'll be at my parent's if you care," she said as she walked out the door.

"Ump. I know that's right," Anthony said under his breath.

He looked up at the television and instantly began to laugh. It was just at that moment that he realized that the television was never on.

"Damn. I'm losing it," he said.

The nurse peeked her head through the door.

"Mr. Lee you okay?" she asked.

"Yes, ma'am, come on in," he said.

The nurse walked in looking around the room.

"Whatcha looking for?" he said.

"Just making sure nothings broke, shattered or hanging from a limb!" she smiled.

"Now, I'm straight. Can't say that about my wife though," he teased.

"Yeah, she seem very upset. Are you crazy to have another woman around when you're wife can see her?" asked the nurse.

"She just wasn't any woman. She's my first love," Anthony announced.

The nurse continued to check Anthony as he spoke.

"Lisa and I have always been tight. And I mean, she came to see me because word got to her. I didn't plan for her to spend the night but I'm glad she did. It felt good," Anthony said.

"That sounds sweet. I won't get in your business, honey, just know that with prayer following your heart won't ever be the wrong decision," she said.

The nurse smiled and walked out the door. Anthony turned on the television and instantly began to fall asleep.

Lisa woke up to the phone ringing in her ear. She tried to ignore it, but it was too loud.

"Hello?" she answered.

"Gurl it's three in the afternoon why you sleep. Ooooohhhhh, you pregnant! Ain't you?" Lynelle yelled in the phone.

"Hell naw! Gurl I'm tired. I slept on a very small hospital bed with Anthony last night," Lisa explained.

"You just can't stay away from that nigga? How's he doing anyway?" Lynelle asked.

"He's okay," Lisa replied.

"Gurl let me tell you!" Lisa began.

"What!?" Lynelle asked excitedly. She pressed her ear against the phone so that she could hear better.

"We chillin' last night and we both fell asleep. When I woke up it was three in the morning and I was about to leave but he asked me to stay. So I did. I go to sleep but I woke up again a few hours later. I didn't want to wake him so I get up and wash up and stuff. I get out of the bath room and ole girl is sitting there about to pass out at the sight of me in her husband's room," Lisa informed her best friend.

"Gurl stop! What happened then?" Lynelle asked.

"It was weird, her face was red, but she cracked a big smile as Anthony introduced us. She shook my hand and thanked me for keeping Anthony company and all. I just hurried and hauled ass," Lisa said.

"Well, damn. What did Anthony do?" Lynelle continued asking questions.

"Gurl he told me that I didn't have to go. That damn boy is crazy." Lisa laughed.

"Gurl, his wife may have killed him. You betta make sure dat ass is still alive! Especially if she had a smile the whole time. And her face as red you said?" Lynelle asked.

"Uh huh," Lisa replied.

"Gurl, she was hot, won't she?" Lynelle laughed.

"Probably. You silly," Lisa teased.

"Naw, she should take care of her man, and she wouldn't have nobody else doing it. So was it good?" Lynelle asked.

"Was what good?" Lisa asked, confused by Lynelle's question.

"The dick!" Lynelle screamed.

"Girl, I didn't sleep with him! The man just had a heart attack. You trying to make me kill him or something?" Lisa stated.

"He would've been one of the happiest dead men around! Gurl can you picture that nigga smiling in his casket!?!" Lynelle laughed in the phone.

"You are silly," Lisa said.

"Oh, for real I know why I called your lazy ass in the first place," Lynelle said.

"Yeah, why?" Lisa asked.

"I heard ole gurl is gay."

"Ole gurl, who?"

"Ant's wife!"

"Shut-up!" Lisa screamed.

"No lie," Lynelle replied.

"How you know? Plus you ain't never seen her. So how you know?" Lisa asked.

"Kim told me she saw her going into Pinky's one night when she was going to Maxwell's across the street."

"Kim who?" Lisa asked.

"Your God sister girl. Wake-up!" Lynelle said.

"I'm up. She don't look gay," Lisa said.

"What you think lesbians are suppose to look butchy or something, like men?" Lynelle asked.

"Naw, but—"

"But nothing, just be quiet," Lynelle teased.

"Wow. That's crazy. That's probably why she wants a divorce," Lisa said.

"What? How you know that?" Lynelle asked.

"Anthony told me. He told me she was telling him that when he had his heart attack," Lisa disclosed.

"Damn. That's fucked up!" Lynelle said.

"Nellie, don't tell nobody okay?" Lisa begged.

"I won't. I promise. But damn. She should have told him. I guess he would have been worst if she had dropped a double whammy on him," Lynelle said.

"Whammy? Who you been around using words like whammy?" Lisa joked.

"Kick rocks Lisa, I'm getting ready to go," Lynelle said.

"Yeah. I'm gonna call Anthony and check on him," Lisa said.

"Okay. Bye," Lynelle said.

"Bye," Lisa replied.

Lisa took a deep breath and dialed the numbers to Anthony's room. The phone rung about three times before he answered.

"Hello?"

"Hey. I was just calling to check on you," Lisa said.

"I'm good. Well great now that I hear your voice," he stated.

"You're a mess. You alone?" Lisa asked.

"In more ways than one," he replied.

"What does that mean?" she questioned.

"I'm ready for something real, Lisa," he responded.

"Oh yeah. Like what?" Lisa asked.

"You and kids," Anthony said.

"You already have a wife and a child," Lisa reminded him.

"Not for long. In a little while I'll just have a son," he said.

"I'm sorry, Ant. So she's going ahead with the proceedings, uh?" Lisa asked.

"Yeah. It's really good for both of us. She deserves someone who can fully love her. I tried a lot of times to be that one but I couldn't. My heart kept rewinding back to you," Anthony said.

"But how? We haven't been exclusive since grade school," Lisa said.

"We've physically been exclusive since grade school but our hearts never stopped being exclusive," Anthony stated.

There was a pause on the phone as both Anthony and Lisa processed Anthony's statement. Inside Lisa agreed. She had always wondered why Anthony's presence was so powerful, even when he wasn't around. She had tried many times to lose the thought of him, but he always seemed to come back to her. Anthony finally broke the silence.

"Look, I don't want to dim your day. I just want to let you know that I am here. I am ready for you and all you have to offer. But that means yo have to be with me and only me. I'm ready for us again," he said.

"How can you say that? I'll be ready when you're really ready. You're still married…remember?" Lisa replied.

"I feel ya. I'm not going anywhere, you're the one who's being offered the contract with the pro-baller!" Anthony teased.

"Ha. You funny," Lisa laughed.

In fact, she had almost forgotten about Rodney.

"By the way, I'll be waiting," Anthony said.

"Okay. I have to go. I'll you later. If you leave today call me," Lisa said.

"I'll do that, but more than likely I won't be leaving until tomorrow," Anthony said.

"I'll call you later then. Get some rest," Lisa said.

"I'll try," Anthony replied.

"Bye, bighead," Lisa said.

"And you know it," Anthony teased.

Lisa hung up the phone, laughing.

"That boy is silly," she said to herself as she dialed Rodney's number.

"Hey, baby, what you doing?" Lisa asked.

"Just got in from practice," he answered.

"What you doing tonight? Can you see me?" Lisa asked.

"Chillin' and naw, I can't see you on the phone. Who you think I am?" Rodney teased.

"No, for real, pookie, I want to see you," Lisa pleaded.

"Ah. I'm sorry I can't. Coach got us on a real strict curfew. It's already about five by the time I come get you, it'll be time to be back by eight," Rodney said apologetically.

Lisa became silent. She thought to herself that she'd rather have her old fiancé back. Ever since he made the pros his time with her has become very short. Rodney allowed the silence to continue for a few moments before he spoke.

"Talk, gurl! Why you so quiet?" he asked.

"No reason. How's practice going?" Lisa asked.

"I don't want to talk about that. I just left it!" Rodney snapped.

"Yuk. What's with you?" Lisa asked.

"Nothing. Look, I'm tired. I'll talk to you later," Rodney said.

Lisa deeply sighed and hung up the phone without a goodbye.

Lisa laid across her bed and began to cry. She did not know what to do. She felt like her life was so worthless she was torn, between security from her fiancé with no real affection and her first love with affection but no real security. Anthony always told her he loved her, but he had a wife and child. Lisa wasn't sure if he could love her the way she felt she deserved to be Lisa continued to hopelessly cry. The phone began to ring, but she ignored it. It stopped and so did Lisa's cries. She sat up on the bed, took a deep breath and headed to the bathroom to wash up. She walked into the bathroom, looked at her face in the mirror and shook her head.

"Damn girl, get it together," she said to herself. She took a wash cloth, held it under the hot water and laid it on her face. Lisa took a deep sigh and felt a little better. As she was attempted to gather her self together her phone rang again. This time she broke through the door and ran to the kitchen to pick up her cordless phone.

"Hello?" Lisa answered.

"Hey Lis, What's up?" Kim asked.

"Just chilling," Lisa said solemnly.

"You lying. What's wrong with you for real?" Kim asked.

Lisa took a deep breath and began to speak.

"Well, let me start out by saying I spent the night at the hospital last night…with Anthony," Lisa said.

She waited for Kim to make her comment, she knew she would.

"Oh my God, you gave the boy butt in the hospital room?" Kim screamed.

"NO! Why is everyone asking me that? I am NOT a HOE!" Lisa screamed.

"Damn gurl calm down. Ain't nobody calling you a hoe!" Kim said.

"Anyway. I'm just mad because I called Rodney, since I hadn't heard from him. I asked could I see him and in more words or so, he told me he didn't have time," Lisa said.

"Ahh Boo-Boo. I'm sorry. I'm gonna help you feel better. I'm gonna come and get you in about an hour," Kim said.

"Kim. I don't feel like going anywhere. Maybe I'll handout wit you when I feel better," Lisa replied.

"Bitch, it ain't bout what you want. I told you be ready in a hour. If you felt good I wouldn't be taking you out! That's the whole point...genius!" Kim teased.

"Fine. I'll be ready," Lisa said.

"Yeah, you betta. Don't wear nothing homely either. I know how you get when you're sad. I refuse to take Miss Pitman out!" Kim teased.

"Miss Pittman, who the hell is that?" Lisa asked.

"Jane Pittman! Don't be dressing like some old lady." Kim laughed.

"Ha, you funny. Oh yeah, by the way my boy here. He want to talk to you!" Lisa said.

"Who's that?" Kim questioned.

"Tone," Lisa responded.

"Tone? Tone who?" Kim asked.

At that point Lisa hung up the phone.

All she could do was laugh. Lisa got up and looked for some clothes to put on. She pulled out a pair of blue Baby Phat jeans and a purple Baby Phat shirt. She took out her purple snake skin pumps. She laid her clothes across the bed and jumped in the shower. As she showered, she thought about all the times she and Rodney showered together, either before or after a wonderful sexual episode.

"Damn, I need some," Lisa said to herself.

She continued to shower thinking how much time she and Rodney used to spend together back when they were at CAU. Between the thoughts of Rodney and the hot water, Lisa began to feel warm wetness between her legs. She looked down and saw the clear silky substance. She shook her head and continued her shower. Once Lisa was fresh, she got out of the shower, dried off and put on her panties and bra. She stood in the mirror as she primped herself. First she moisturized her body with warm vanilla body lotion. Then she began to put mousse in her hair for shine and curls. Lastly, she cleaned up and shaped her eyebrows. She looked in the mirror at her self and smiled.

"There. That's better."

She smiled again at herself and then winked. She left the bathroom and walked into her room to dress. As soon as she slipped on her last shoe and began to put on her jewelry, she heard Kim coming through the door.

"Heffa? Heff-a!" Kim yelled.

"I know I shouldn't have given you a key. You psycho path!" Lisa screamed at her.

"Aw be quiet!" Kim said walking through Lisa's bedroom door. She stood stunned.

"Look at you...foxy momma! You just can't get our of heels, uh?" she teased.

"Nope, you just jealous! I look good in my pumps!" Lisa said.

Lisa turned around in a circle and stopped and posed.

"Diva let's go! I don't have time for you to be dancing around the room when we could be in a real club dancing," Kim joked.

"Where we going?" Lisa asked as they were walking out of the apartment to Kim's car.

The girls got in the car and headed to their destination.

"Oh, you not gonna answer my question?" Lisa asked.

"What question? You know I don't listen well," Kim said.

"Where are we going?" Lisa asked again.

"Maxwell's," Kim answered.

Lisa sat back and thought about the last time she had actually been to a real club. She had been to Tony's but that wasn't a real club.

"What's wrong with you? Why are you so quiet?" Kim asked.

"I have a lot of things on my mind," Lisa replied.

"Well you might as well get them off your mind, because we gonna have a good time!" Kim said.

Lisa looked out the window as Kim parked in the lot of Maxwell's.

"Wow, there's a lot of people here," Lisa said.

She watched all the women go in with mini skirts, short dresses, booty shorts and all. She laughed to herself.

"What's so funny?" Kim asked.

"It's funny how all these women with different crazy stuff on and you see them with the same shoes...open toe stilettos, very high boots or flats with rhinestones! Yuk. If you ever see me with those flat, shiny shoes on in public, punch me!" Lisa said.

Kim parked and turned off the car. She pulled down the visor and began to freshen her make-up in the mirror.

"You fly, you don't have to freshen up!" Lisa teased.

"You betta look at your face!" Kim replied.

Lisa pulled down the visor in front of her.

"What's wrong with my face?" Lisa asked.

She tried to find out what the problem was.

"Besides the fact that you ugly?" Kim laughed.

"Oh, you got jokes, hater!" Lisa responded.

Lisa touched up her gloss. Meshed her lips together and then smiled.

"Oh, please get out of the mirror!" Kim said.

Kim and Lisa stepped out of the car and headed for the entrance of the club.

"Wow, a line," Lisa said.

They walked and stood in the line. After a few moments one of the huge bouncers at the beginning of the line walked over to Kim and Lisa.

"Lisa? Lisa Jones, what's up cutie? You remember me?" the bouncer asked.

Lisa looked at the man up and down and then the memory popped in her head.

"Shawn? Oh my. Boy you are big, how are you?' Lisa screamed.

Lisa held her arms out to hug him, but instead her picked Lisa up and spun around with her in his arms.

"Gurl. Where have you been?" Shawn asked.

"Well I went away to school, but—"

"Hump. Um," Kim interrupted.

Lisa knew exactly what that noise was for, so she introduced the two.

"Shawn this is my sister Kim and Kim this is Shawn. He went to school with me, Anthony and David," Lisa said.

"Nice to meet you Shawn," Kim said, shaking his hand.

"Like wise sexy. Yeah, Lisa I heard you hit the lottery," Shawn said.

Lisa looked at him confused but Kim instantly began to snicker.

"What are you talking about?" Lisa asked.

"You know," Kim said.

Lisa looked around then at Shawn.

"Damn, is this line moving at all?" she hinted.

"Oh, my bad. I was so wrapped up in taking to you and your fine ass, sista. Get out of this line and follow me," Shawn said, directing the girls to the VIP line. Kim looked at Lisa and winked. Lisa leaned over and whispered in Kim's ear.

"You know your sister knows how to take care of you," Lisa said.

The girls followed Shawn into the club to a blocked off area. He stopped at a plush seated booth.

"Here you go ladies. I gave you my personal booth. I hope you enjoy. I'll be checking on you periodically through the night. What ever you want, order it through Cindy and she'll put it on my tab," Shawn said.

He began to walk away when Kim stopped him.

"Shawn," Kim called.

He turned around and looked directly into Kim's eyes.

"Don't forget to come back. I would love to have a drink and dance with you," Kim said.

"Oh, no doubt, lady. Why wouldn't I? You sitting at my booth," he responded.

"I'll be waiting," Kim said with a flirtatious smile.

Shawn walked away leaving Kim and Lisa alone to enjoy and observe the club's atmosphere.

"Any more and your lips would have automatically been around ole boy's Johnson," Lisa said, laughing.

"What are you talking about?" Kim innocently asked.

"Oh you know. I'll be waiting," Lisa said, mocking Kim.

Both women laughed at the mockery. Cindy walked up to the table with a bottle of Moet chilling in a ice filled canister and two Champagne glasses.

"Compliments of Shawn. You girls ready to order?" Cindy asked.

"Are you Cindy?" Kim asked, looking the waitress up and down.

"Oh my goodness. I didn't introduce myself?" Cindy asked.

Kim and Lisa looked at each other and answered, "No," in unison.

"I'm so sorry, I've been running all night. My name is Cindy and I'll be taking care of you tonight! And probably ever night if Shawn has you sitting in his booth," she said.

"Really," Kim asked.

"Yes. He doesn't invite many people outside his family to his booth. Now what can I get you to eat?" Cindy asked.

"Well Cindy, we haven't had a chance to look at the menus. Can you give us a minute or two?" Kim asked.

"Sure thing. Here you go," Cindy said, handing Kim a two way pager.

"What's that for?" Lisa asked.

"Shawn and the other bouncers I work for, have two ways for their tables so you can page me when you need me. They said it cuts out the unnecessary interruptions," Cindy explained.

Lisa and Kim looked at each other in amazement.

"Oh, Okay. We'll do that," Kim said.

"Okay, Thanks," Cindy said.

Lisa couldn't get over what Cindy said so she stopped before she got away.

"Hey Cindy, let me ask you. Why have you been running around so much if you have the two way?" Lisa asked.

"Well, one of the other bouncer's brother is having a party and they have been running me rampid!" Cindy said.

"Damn, well do your thang, girl!" Kim said.

Cindy walked away. Lisa looked at Kim and smiled.

"Thank you for bringing me out, sis."

"No problem. I never want to see you down," Kim responded.

Kim got up from the booth and kneeled in the chair to look over into the crowd of people in club. Her eyes were immediately directed to someone who looked familiar. She squinted her eyes for a better focus.

"Oh no," Kim said under her breath, but Lisa heard her.

"What? What's going on out there?" Lisa asked.

"Um, girl, nothing," Kim lied.

She quickly sat down and gathered her thoughts. By that time Cindy had returned with two mixed drinks. Kim grabbed one glass and pushed the other to Lisa.

"Drink up!" Kim said clinging her glass to Lisa's for a toast.

Kim was trying to figure to ways keep her sister from knowing that her fiancé was at the club not in his room.

Chapter 13

Lisa noticed Kim acting real funny. She kept looking over the back of the chair like she was keeping her eye on something.

"Girl. What is wrong with you?" Lisa asked.

"What are you talking about?" Kim asked.

"You keep looking over that chair like you spying on a cheating boyfriend or something," Lisa said.

Kim's eyes almost popped out her head as she turned to face Lisa and think of a quick lie.

"Oh, naw, I'm just scoping out the place, looking at all the fine men in here!" Kim lied.

"Well turn around and sit down. You suppose to be helping me," Lisa groaned.

"I know. You ready to order?" Kim asked, holding the menu up, pretending to read it. Lisa picked up her menu and looked over the menu. She decided to order the wings. She placed the menu down and looked at Kim.

"What?" Kim shouted.

"I want wings, hot. Ranch dressing and extra celery," Lisa responded.

"Bitch, who I look like, Cindy?" Kim teased.

"Naw, but you can two-way her," Kim said.

"Fine," Kim said.

She took the two way out and paged Cindy. She then turned around and looked over the seat again. She looked at the dance floor. She saw Rodney dancing with a girl like he had no care in the world. Kim huffed and puffed. She turned back around.

"What is wrong with you?" Lisa asked.

"Nothing," Kim lied.

"Look, I'm tired of asking you what is wrong and then you telling me nothing," Lisa said.

Kim was saved by the pager. Cindy came rushing to the table with the food.

"Okay ladies. Wing, hot with ranch dressing and celery for you," she said, placing the plate in front of Lisa.

"And shrimp and fries for you," Cindy said, placing the plate in front of Kim.

Kim and Lisa both looked at their plates and inhaled the aroma.

"Thank yo so much," Lisa said.

"Yeah, Thanks," Kim said, smacking her lips.

"No problem, girls. I'll be back with more drinks." Cindy smiled and rushed off. Lisa began to eat her food, wondering why her God sister was behaving so funny and why her fiancé has begun to act as if he has a huge crown on his head. Silence fell on the table as the two women ate. Lisa could not bare to keep her feelings locked inside.

"You know, ever since Rodney got this pro-deal, he has been acting like he is the shit. I mean the pure shit. He has never treated me like an outsider. I mean he is really acting like he the shit!" Lisa said deeply sighing.

"Well, maybe he's trying to cope with things. This is new for him. He don't know what to expect. Maybe you should give him the benefit of the doubt," Kim attempted to soothe Lisa.

"What ever! I wonder what Tony's doing?" Lisa said aloud.

He eyes became extra wide when she realize what she had said out loud. Lisa dropped her head and continued to eat her food.

"Lisa don't be ashamed, it's easy to feel unwanted when a man devotes much of the time, previously given to you, somewhere else. But you have to decide what you want to do. You have to make decisions for you," Kim responded.

Lisa looked at Kim and gulped down her third glass of Moet.

"Let me see that two way," Lisa demanded.

Kim looked at Lisa in a confused manner and relentlessly handed Lisa the pager. Lisa typed and handed it back.

"What you order?" Kim asked.

"A double shot of Patron," Lisa replied.

"Damn, you trying to be on your ass?" Kim asked.

"Naw, just trying to relax and the Mo not doing it fast enough for me," Lisa said.

"Well, you need to be careful with the drinking," Kim said.

Cindy walked over with Lisa's shots.

"Here you go. You ladies know this stuff is really strong, don't you?" she said.

"Oh, it's all for Shera over there!" Kim teased.

"Yelp and I'll take it," Lisa said.

Lisa picked up the first shot glass and shot it straight down.

"Woooo," Lisa screamed.

Kim and Cindy looked in amazement. She then took a deep breath and gulped it down with one gulp.

"Grrrrr. I'm done," she growled.

"And you should be. You're gonna pass out!" Kim said.

Cindy continued her stare, shook the excitement off and collected the empty dishes off the table and walked away.

"Girl that waitress thinks you're crazy, you know that don't you?" Kim said.

"Yeah? She'll be alright," Lisa said, getting up.

"Where the hell you going?" Kim asked.

Lisa clapped her hands to the music.

"Wew, I'm getting ready to dance," Lisa shouted.

Kim got up to follow her when it dawned on her that Rodney was on the floor acting like he was single and free.

"Why don't we wait a while?" Kim stalled.

"Hell naw, I want to dance and I want to dance now," Lisa demanded.

Lisa rushed to the dance floor. Kim hurried behind her, praying that Rodney would be no where around. She reached Lisa at the edge of the dance floor dancing alone but enjoying it. She stood by her side and searched the dance floor for Rodney. She looked all over the floor but could not see him. Lisa was in her own little world.

"I'm gonna roam the floor," Kim shouted over the music.

"Girl, go head, I'm cool right here," Lisa insisted.

Kim hesitated before she walked off. She wanted to make sure she saw Rodney before Lisa did. She did not want her sister to be hurt. She walked through the crowds of people dancing but did not see Rodney.

"Maybe get came to his damn senses and left," Kim said to herself.

"Damn. Do all fine women talk to themselves?" Shawn shouted and startled Kim.

Kim quickly turned around and grabbed her chest.

"Boy are you crazy? You scared me to death!" Kim shouted.

"My bad shawty. But for real, who you taking to?" Shawn teased.

"Myself," Kim embarrassedly smiled.

"Should I walk away now?" Shawn asked.

"No, I'm okay, for real," Kim assured Shawn.

Shawn took a step back, looked at Kim and smiled.

"Gurl, let's dance," he said, grabbing her hand and leading Kim to the middle of the dance floor.

"I can't I have to check on Lisa," Kim shouted, attempting to pull away.

"I just saw her. She okay. Dancing wit some dude over there," Shawn said, pointing to the side of the dance floor where Kim left Lisa.

Kim was still somewhat resistant. She stopped walking. Shawn stopped also.

"You gonna be difficult? Do I need to go about my business?" Shawn asked.

"No, but—" Kim attempted to explain, but Shawn picked her up and carried her to the middle of the dance floor.

"Boy, you are crazy. What's wrong with you," Kim asked in his ear.

"Nothing, I think I found my wife," Shawn said.

"Where, let me see her!" Kim teased.

She was flattered but did not make it known.

As soon as Shawn and Kim arrived to their destination, "Before I Let You Go" by Frankie Beverly and Maze blasted through the speaker.

"Ah, shit. That's my jam," Shawn yelled.

Kim laughed and smiled so much that her face hurt as she danced.

Before the song finished Kim and Shawn heard loud screams.

"What the hell, I can't even take a break. Niggas don't eva know how to act. Damn!" Shawn shouted.

He leaned over Kim and kissed her on the top of her head.

"I'll catch you later. Duty calls," Shawn said, rushing through the crowd.

Kim walked on the opposite side of the floor, away from the chaos. She slowly walked around and then stopped. She looked to see the people rushing to the edge of the dance floor.

"People please lets break it up and act decent!" the deejay screamed through the mic.

Kim stood and thought about all the possible reasons people would be fighting at the club. She thought about the typical thugs showing off. People fighting over money. Just as she thought about two men fighting over a chick who probably don't want them, a light bulb went off in her head.

"Oh shit, Lisa," Kim yelled, busting through the crowd.

Once she arrived to the scene she saw Lisa walking away.

"Lisa?" she called out.

Lisa stopped and looked at Kim. She looked towards the crowd.

"Look at his ass Kim, he talking about going to bed and his lying high and mighty ass ova here dancing and singing to some random bitch!" Lisa yelled.

Kim turned to her right to see Rodney looking at Lisa with a very pretty girl standing behind him, but close enough to disclose the fact they were together.

"Lisa!" Rodney called.

Lisa stuck her middle finger out at Rodney.

Rodney turned to Kim.

"Kim take your sister home. She's had too much to drink," he said.

Kim looked at Lisa.

"Hold on babe. Let me say something. I'll meet you at the door," Kim said.

Lisa stood for a second and looked at Kim. Kim gave Lisa her *it's okay* stare. Lisa rolled her eyes at Rodney and the unfamiliar woman before heading for the door.

"Okay, people. Let's get this party back and rolling," the deejay announced.

The crowd began to regain their party status. Shawn walked over to Kim, who was now standing in front of Rodney.

"You okay, sexy?" he asked.

"Yeah, I'm cool," Kim said, not taking her eyes off of Rodney and the woman.

"Man, that's fucked up," Shawn said to Rodney before walking off.

Kim waited for Shawn to walk off before she began to speak.

"You know? The only reason why she was here is because I told her she needed to get some air from crying because you told her you were too tired to see her. Ain't that some shit?!" Kim yelled.

Rodney attempted to speak but Kim stopped him.

"Hold on. I ain't Lisa. That's some fucked up shit for real. You ain't even been pro for a month and you cheating wit groupies already!"

The woman behind Rodney stepped to his side. She opened her mouth as is she were going to speak.

"Bitch don't think about it!" Kim sternly said.

Kim looked back at Rodney.

"Let me finish so I can get to my sister. That girl been there wit you before you were anybody! And I bet your gold digging ass didn't know he was engaged!" Kim yelled at the woman.

"Kim tell your sister I'll call her when she calm down!" Rodney said.

"Nigga Pleez. You betta come more correct than that or yo feelings gonna get hurt. You better decide if you want to have a wife and family like you begged my sister for or some disease from fucking with dez jump offs!" Kim said.

She began to walk off but stopped. She turned around and walked back towards Rodney.

"By the way, I forgot one more thang," she said.

To Rodney and Kim's surprise, the mysterious woman spoke.

"Now what? Don't you think you've said enough? Let the nigga decide what he want. Don't know body want to hear no mo sob statements for your sister," she bravely said.

Rodney's eyes opened wide. He looked at the woman and then at Kim. He took one step to the side away from the woman.

"Just as I thought. I knew I should have said all I had to say!" im calmly said to Kim took a step back and punched the woman in her nose. The woman grabbed her nose, but not quickly enough to stop the blood from gushing from it.

"Get your fucking mind right hoe!" Kim yelled at her.

Kim headed to the door yelling,

"Bitches always want to bring the ghetto out my ass!"

Kim busted through the front door to see Lisa and Shawn laughing against the glass.

"Oh my goodness girl you laid her ass out!" Lisa yelled.

"Shera, you okay?" Shawn asked.

"Yeah, no body fronts on my sister and I knew she had lip so before that bitch could talk some untruth shit, I let her think about some things," Kim said.

"Damn, take a breath," Shawn said.

Kim took a deep breath and looked at Shawn.

"I'm sorry," she apologized.

"You good. Here's my card. Take your sister home. Y'all have some coca, eat some popcorn and watch Waiting to Exhale or some shit like that," he said, handing her the car.

"Waiting to Exhale?" Lisa said, laughing.

"Yeah, ain't that what y'all do when y'all mad?" Shawn asked.

Kim and Lisa both laughed at Shawn's statement.

Lisa looked down at her watch and back at Shawn.

"Naw, I'm going to sleep, but my sister will call you." She winked.

Kim stood and smiled while her sister tried her best to hook her up with Shawn.

"You make sure she does. And don't worry about Rodney, he'll come to his senses!" Shawn said to Lisa.

"I'm not worried. He knows he's in deep shit and it'll take a huge saver to get him from this one," Lisa said.

"See you later, Shawn," Kim said.

"I hope sooner!" he replied.

"C'mon corny!" Lisa said, pulling Kim towards the car.

When they reached the car, both woman remained quiet. No one seemed to be breathing, let alone talking until thy reached Lisa's apartment.

"You staying with me tonight?" Lisa asked.

"Yeah. It's late, plus I'm gonna call Shawn and maybe invite him over," Kim replied.

"Why you gotta do that here?" Lisa asked, getting out of the car.

"Because you know him more than I do," Kim replied, continuing the conversation through the door.

"But damn. Don't be having sex with him yet!" Lisa said.

"Hey. I don't tell you what to do!" Kim laughed.

"Whatever," Lisa said, going into the room and closing the door. Kim walked into the guest room and opened the closet.

"Nice to see you kept my emergency move in stash of clothing and shoes," Kim yelled.

"Bitch I'm throwing it away tomorrow!" Lisa teased.

Lisa walked out her room and to the bath room.

"Hurry up too. I don't want cold water when I take a shower!" Kim yelled.

"You don't pay no water here," Lisa yelled back.

"You don't either!" Kim yelled once more.

As soon as Kim heard the water turn on, the phone rang. Kim looked at the clock on the cable box. "Who the hell calling at this time of night," she whispered.

She answered the phone.

"Hello?" Kim said.

"Who dis?" the voice asked.

Rodney?" Kim asked.

"Yeah, where Lisa at Kim?" Rodney asked.

"Boy, you know betta. She ain't calmed down by now. You hurt that girl," Kim said.

"Well, just tell her I called," Rodney said.

"Yeah, I will," Kim said.

Kim hung up the phone and took her clothes out for bed. Lisa walked out of the bathroom.

"I hope I have some hot water," Kim said, walking pass Lisa

and rushing into the bathroom. She closed the door but opened it back up.

"Girl. Rodney called. He told me to tell you he called," she said and closed the door again.

Lisa grunted and took her cell phone out of her purse to place it on the charger. She looked down at it when it beeped. The phone indicated that she had a new text message. She pressed the button to reveal the message. It was from Rodney. It read:

Lisa, please call me when
You calm down. I really do
Love you and didn't mean
To hurt you. I know I fucked
Up, but please for give me.

Rodney

Lisa looked at the phone shook her head and deleted the message. She knelt down to say her prayers.

"Lord, please help me to decide what to do with Rodney. I love him so much, but he is changing. He's not the man I used to know. If he's gonna let this football career get to his head, I don't want to be with him. Why can't men just be satisfied wit what they have, especially if it's good? Is it me Lord? Am I wring? I know I have explored since Rodney and I have been together but I just want to make sure marring him is best. Lord please guide me! In Jesus name I pray. Amen."

Lisa got up and crawled into her bed wiping the tears that had fallen. She slid deep into the bed. She heard Kim walk away from the bath room and into the guest room, but that was the last thing she heard before she fell asleep.

Chapter 14

I still couldn't believe I was still lying in this damn hospital bed. I was so tired of niggas walking in and out asking me questions and feeling sorry for me. I looked over to see David asleep in the chair and the television on ESPN. I don't remember changing it from the news so I must have fell asleep. I moved to let David know I was awake.

"Hey nigga you alright?" David asked, shifting in the chair.

"Yeah, I'm cool," I said.

"Oh," he responded looking at the television.

"Did the doctor come in here? How long I been sleep?" I asked.

"Yeah, he left that paper on the table right there. He said he didn't want to wake you and that he'll see you in the morning. He said you needed rest, too," David replied.

I grabbed the paper and began to read it. It was a summary of what happened to me, what they did to help me and how I needed to care for myself when I was discharged.

"How long I been sleep?" I asked, placing the papers back on the table.

"A few hours. It's probably about time for the nurse to come back in here to check you. You must've been tired because she came in here at first loud and shit, right beside you and you didn't budge," David said.

I didn't know what he was talking about, but I know I didn't remember anything but the news. Just as I began to sit up on the bed the nurse rushed in with her cart.

"Hey Mr. Lee, how are you today?" she asked.

"I will be fine if you stop messing with me," I answered.

"I know, we can be irritating. It's okay. You don't offend me, by telling me that," she said.

She took out her thermometer and took my temperature.

"Uh, huh," she said, recording the reading.

She then looked at the monitor I was hooked up to, recorded the readings from that, pushed some buttons and looked at me.

"You cold?" she asked.

"Not really. What kind of question is that? I'm laying up in a hospital bed with a gown on my ass out. And you ask me if I'm cold!" I responded.

She looks at me for a moment and then over at David.

"You have a slight temp. I just wanted to see if you were having any side affects from that," she said.

"Oh, naw, I'm not that cold. So I got a fever, what does that mean?" I asked.

"Well I'll give you a fever reducer and see what that does. It could mean a few things. You could have an infection, you could be having a response to the meds we have you on going through your IV or you could just be catching a cold from being in this room," she said.

She gathered her things and began to walk out of the door.

"I'll check on you later Mr. Lee. Press the button if you need anything," she said.

"I need a glass of Henny, you got that?" he asked.

"No, I'm sorry, we don't serve that here," she responded.

"Well, I'll be fine then," I said.

She walked out of the door.

"Man, what the hell is wrong with you? You know she ain't got no liquor, but she got ass! I would've asked her for that before some liquor," David said.

I laughed. "Yeah that's cause you a pervert!" I said.

I got up to use the bathroom.

"Damn, cover up or some shit. I don't want to see all of that," David yelled.

"Shut-the-hell-up!" I yelled back closing the door after me.

I hated using the bathroom in the hospital room. The fan was just so damn loud that it was hard to concentrate on the business at hand. I didn't know if they were putting stuff in my food or not. All I know was I kept going to the bathroom like I had to go, only to sit in there and have nothing happen. After fifteen minutes I got up and walked out. I washed my hands and turned to get back in the bed. To my surprise Jamaal and Maria was there. When I looked at Jamaal he was in the bed and had the covers pulled over his head.

"Hey man, who's that in my bed?" I asked David.

Jamaal giggled from underneath the covers.

"I don't now man, maybe it's nobody. Why don't you just get in the bed and lay on what ever it is," David teased.

Jamaal jumped out the bed

"Nooooo don't lay on me, Daddy!" he yelled.

"Oh, it was you, Mal? In my bed!?" I asked.

Jamaal shook his head, yes, laughing. He ran over and gave me a big hug.

"Hold on, man, you trying to know me over?" I asked.

"No, Daddy. You sick?" he asked.

"I'm okay, baby. Who told you that?" I said, glancing at Maria.

"Mommie," he said.

Still not acknowledging Maria's presence, I got back in the bed and motioned for Jamaal to lay beside me.

"Daddy, you want to go home?" he asked.

"Yes," I responded.

"Today?" he asked.

"I want to, but probably tomorrow!" I answered.

"Tomar?" he asked.

I shook my head in agreement. The response must have satisfied him because he did not question me about going home anymore. He laid beside me talking to David and watching television.

"Um. Hello Anthony, how are you?" Maria asked.

"I'm okay. You said that like you expected me to speak. You walked into my room," I said.

"Yeah, whatever. Your son wanted to see you," she said.

I just looked at her and then at Jamaal.

"You wanted to see me, man?" I asked Jamaal.

"Yep," he responded.

"I'm glad. Daddy missed you," I said.

"I miss you, Daddy," he said. Jamaal got on his knees and kissed me.

"C'mon, Mal, let's get a snack from downstairs," David said.

Although I hated what he was doing, he left anyway. I did not want to be in the room alone with Maria. As far as I was concerned, we were done. David and Jamaal left out of the room, closing the door behind them. Maria walked over to the chair beside the window, where David had been sitting, and sat down. I looked at the television.

"So where's your little girlfriend?" she asked.

I took a deep breath and blew it out. "I'm not gonna go there with you. She is just a friend who's concerned about me," I said.

"Ump. Just a friend, she was in the bed with you. Friends don't sleep in the same bed. Especially those of the opposite sex without something going on," she said.

The conversation was so funny. It was like listening to Lisa a few years back when she started noticing Maria spending more time with me and she reacted the same way. I kept looking at the television.

"Did you hear me?" she asked.

"Yeah. But what you want me to say? She said the same thing about you back in the day," I said and smiled to myself.

"Oh, yeah, but she isn't married to you. I am," she said.

"But don't want to be," I said.

"Neither do you. We shouldn't talk about this now. We should wait until you better," she said.

"I'm good. Let's discuss it now!" I demanded.

"No, I rather not," she said.

"Fine," I responded.

At that very moment David and Jamaal returned with bags of chips and soda.

"Man, why you give him all that junk?" I asked.

"Daddy, it's good. Not junk…chips," he said.

"Oh, really?" I asked.

"Uh, huh. I got soda, too," Jamaal said, showing me his bottle.

"Did you tell Cousin David thank you?" I asked.

"Yes. Thank you," Jamaal said.

"No problem, man," David said.

"Jamaal, you ready to leave?" Maria asked, moving towards the door.

"I go bye-bye, Daddy," Jamaal said.

"Okay man, I'll see you later, okay? I love you," I said.

He followed Maria out the door. She left without saying goodbye. David felt the tension.

"What you do to that gurl?" David asked.

"I didn't do anything. Why am I always at fault?" I asked.

"Homegirl was out. She ain't say bye or nothing," David teased.

"Yeah, she'll get over it," I said.

"So what did the doctor say on those paper?" he asked.

"I'll be here at least until tomorrow evening, but I won't count on it," I said.

"Why not?" he asked.

"Cause they talking about running a few more test. And you

know that when the lab people come it be so late that waiting for the results and doctors response takes you to the next day," I said.

"Aww, man," David responded.

"Do me a favor?" I asked.

"What?" he asked.

"Get my car and bring it up here so I can leave when they do let me," I said.

"Aight. I'm bout to be out, but I'll get Danny to follow me over tomorrow," David said.

"Okay. You going out?" I asked.

"Yeah, me and Rita going to dinner," he said.

"What! Not you and the lady!" I teased.

"Yeah, man gotta keep her mouth closed," David said.

"Nigga stop playing, you now you gonna marry that girl," I said.

"Don't know about all that," he said, getting up to walk out the room. He walked over to the bed and gave me a pound.

"One," he said.

"Aight. Have a nuff drinks, food and pussy for me nigga," I said.

"Get your own!" David teased, walking out the door.

I laid back and thought about what I'd do when I got home. Lisa popped in my head. I wondered what she was doing. I closed my eyes and pictured her arms around me. Just as she was about to kiss me, the phone rung. I cleared my voice and answered.

"Hello?"

"Don't try to sound sexy for me, boy I seen your little booty," my mother teased on the other end.

"Hey ma. How you doing?" I asked.

"I'm good baby. The better question is how are you?" she asked.

"I'm okay, Ma. I'm ready to leave. I'm so tired of being here," I whined to my mother.

"I know, baby. It'll get better. You'll be home soon," my momma said.

"Thanks, Ma. I'm gonna try to rest," I lied.

"Okay baby, I'll call you later," she said.

I hung up the phone thinking about what Lisa was doing.

Chapter 15

Rodney woke up feeling tired like he had practiced all night long. He sat up on the bed and looked around. The environment was unfamiliar to him. He didn't know where he was or how he got there. He jumped out of the bed and rushed to put on his clothes, which were on the floor beside the bed. Just as he completed putting on his last piece of clothing a female appeared at the entrance of the room.

"Surpris—where are you going? I thought we'd have breakfast in bed," she announced, looking confused as to why Rodney was fully clothed.

Rodney attempted to walk out of the room but he young lady would not move away from the door.

"Look, sweetheart, I don't mean no harm but I gotta go. I got fiancé and she probably wondering where I am," Rodney demanded.

"Well, I don't think she'll have a problem remembering that," the woman stated as she walked over to the night stand and placed the breakfast tray down. When she turned around to see Rodney's face, it was just as she had expected. His mouth was wide open and his eyes matched to a tee.

"Wha-what's that suppose to mean?" he stuttered.

"You don't remember baby?" she smiled.

"Hell naw. What the hell you talking 'bout?" Rodney asked, getting louder.

"No need to raise your voice. Seems like you made your decision at the club and I think your little girl-friend got the message," she said.

Rodney stood for a couple of seconds and spoke.

"I don't now what you talking about. You pretty and all...I mean considering—"

"Considering what?" the woman interrupted.

"Considering you look like somebody knocked the shit out of you! What happened? Who lumped our nose like that?" Rodney asked.

"Nigga you got jokes? You won't worried bout my lumped nose when you were fucking me last night," the woman yelled.

"Look, I didn't mean to upset you, I gotta go," Rodney said.

He began to walk around the apartment to find his way out when he stopped at a photo on the wall.

"Who's that nigga?" Rodney asked.

"Why?" she asked.

"Naw, he look like a nigga I seen before," Rodney said.

"You don't know him," the woman said.

"You probably right. Fuck! What am I saying? I don't even know your ass. Who are you? What's your name?" he asked.

"We went through this last night. If you don't remember, sorry for you!" she said.

"Sorry? Bitch please. It don't matter!" he said.

"Bitch...oh, okay...like that. Let me show you to the door. I got what I wanted anyway!" she said opening the front door.

"Cool. Holla," Rodney said, walking out the door and towards his car.

"Sooner than you think...but I won't be the one, holla'n," the woman said under her breath while closing the door.

Rodney got in his car and tried to regain his senses. He began to pull out the apartment complex. After five minutes of driving, he realized where he was. He was down the street from the club.

"Damn it Rodney, get your head right," he yelled.

He looked at the clock on the dash board. It read 7:00am. He took a deep sigh and picked up his cell phone to call Lisa. He dialed the number and waited for her to pick up. After a few rings she answered.

"Hello?" Lisa whispered.

"Baby, what's going on?" Rodney said, hoping to lighten the mood until he found out what happened last night.

"Oh, hell naw. How you gonna call me like shit ain't hit the damn fan last night?" Lisa screamed.

Before Rodney could give his side, she hung up the phone.

"Hello? Hello?" Rodney yelled.

Rodney took a deep breath once more and called back. This time a different person answered.

"Hello?" Kim said, sounding irritated.

"Kim?" Rodney questioned.

"Yeah. What?" she answered.

"Yo, where Lisa at?" he asked.

"I would say she ain't here, but since we both know she is at seven something in the morning, I'll tell you the truth...she don't want to talk to you," Kim said.

"Look, what happened last night?" Rodney asked.

"You don't remember?" Kim gasped.

"If I did I wouldn't have asked you," Rodney snapped.

"Look, don't get a 'tude with me, you the one who need answers, but first...let me ask you this...who'd you wake up with?" she asked.

"No one," Rodney quickly lied.

"Yeah anyway, nigga. Let me make this short so I can go back to sleep and you can stop lying. You told Lisa you won't coming to see her because you were tired. I talked her into going to the club. We saw you there with a chick that looked real familiar, but I can't place her as of right now. Lisa yelled and screamed. You told me to take her home because she had too much to drink. Your gurl ran off at the mouth. I popped her ass and now you begging. Thought you were betta than that…Holla!" Kim yelled and hung up the phone.

Rodney was baffled by the news he had received. He didn't know what to do. The only thing he could think about was seeing Lisa. He lifted his shirt and sniffed. His shirt smelled like someone had sprayed Victoria's secret all over it. He headed to the training dorm to freshen up and change clothes.

When Rodney arrived to the dorm his team mate Jessie was sitting on the edge of the bed watching television.

"Sup?" Rodney said, taking his things out to prepare for a much needed shower.

"Nothing. I should be asking you that! Gone all night and shit," Jessie replied.

"Not now, man. I got some shit I need to handle," Rodney said, heading for the door.

"Well, don't be needing to handle to much shit…coach called an emergency practice today," Jessie informed Rodney.

"What? What the hell…What for? When?" Rodney asked.

"It's at nine until eleven," he said.

"Damn! That's in an hour," Rodney snarled, looking at his watch.

"Yeah, so what ever you had to do will have to get done after practice. You know coach T don't play that missing practice shit," Jessie said.

"Yeah, I know that's right…DAMN!" Rodney yelled, walking back to his bunk, throwing his clothes, soap and towels down and getting out his practice gear.

"Damn, you seem real upset, that girl must have you shook all the way up," Jessie said.

Rodney sat on his bunk and stared into space.

"Now, I think I messed up," Rodney said, leaning back on the bunk to recap what had happened at the club and how he ended up in another woman's bed.

"Okay Mr. Lee, you're all clear to go home. Do you need anything before you go?" the nurse asked, looking at me.

I wanted to tell her I needed some good loving but I figured it wouldn't have mattered.

"Naw, I'm fine. I just don't want t be up in here and thank GOD I am leaving," I said to her.

She handed me my discharge papers to sign. I signed them and handed her, her copy.

"Thank you, you have a safe and healthy life. Remember…take an easy. You don't want to over do your first couple of days back home," the nurse reminded me.

I nodded in agreement and headed out the hospital door. I stepped out of the door and was met by the warm summer's breeze that I missed being in the hospital. I glanced around the parking lot and spotted my car in one of the few parking spaces that was not especially reserved for the handicapped or expected mothers.

"Good looking Dave," I said to myself, walking towards the car.

I got into the car and turned the ignition. Out of no where I was blasted by the sounds of Lil Jon screaming, "Yeeeeaaaahhhh," over Usher as he crooned for his lady to, "Tell me again."

"This nigga is trying to kill me!" I said, turning the radio down. I pulled out of the parking lot heading towards my apartment. I was enjoying being out of the hospital so much that I hadn't even noticed that it was well into the afternoon. I arrived home in no time. I got out of the car and walked in to my home. I closed the door behind me and announced that I was home.

"Hello? Anybody home…cause I am," I screamed.

"Daaadddyyyy," Jamaal screamed as he ran from the back of the apartment.

He ran into my arms and hugged me like he never had.

"Hey, buddy. What's up?" I asked.

As I hugged and kissed my son, Maria walked out of our bed room and stood in the hallway. She stood still for a few moments and then walked towards me and Jamaal.

"Nice to have you home, Ant," she said, giving me a hug.

I was so shocked I actually hugged her back. It felt good though. We hadn't embarrassed each other in such a way since we were at boot camp. She released the embrace, stepped back and kissed me. I thought to myself, *Damn if Dave didn't try to kill me by giving me a heart attack from the loud music and now Ri trying to finish me off!* I stepped back and smiled.

"What's that for?" she asked.

"What?" I asked.

"That smile. You okay?" Maria said.

"I'm trying to figure out what all the affection is for," I responded.

"What a chick can't be happy to see her husband, especially since he's home from the hospital," she said, smiling.

I looked at her very curiously and shrugged my shoulders.

"I guess," I said.

"Daddy, look what me and Mommy did for you," Jamaal said, grabbing me by the hand and leading me to the kitchen. I walked in and saw a cake that had *Welcome Home* scribbled on the top with Jamaal's hand and finger prints all around it.

"That's nice, son. Did you try to taste the cake, man?" I asked, rubbing his head.

"I ate the icing, Daddy," he responded.

"Was it good?" I asked.

"Uh, huh," he responded.

I laughed as I headed towards the bedroom. I got to the entrance and was greeted by balloons, flowers and cards. I looked around in amazement.

"Whatcha just standing here for? I know they told you to come home and rest so go get in the bed. The sheets are brand new and waiting for you!" Maria said with a touch of excitement in her voice.

Now I knew that this was just the calm before the storm. And although I felt that something really fishy was going on I received her generosity, just in case her cold little heart had a bit of sincerity in it for me. I took off my clothes and put on the pajama pants she had laid on the bed for me. I crawled into the bed and turned on the television. I had not noticed that Maria had left the doorway of the room until she reappeared.

"You hungry?" she asked.

"A little," I replied.

"What you got a taste for?" she asked.

I was feeling horny so I decided to try my luck. *I mean, what the hell, she is around and she still is my wife!*

"Pizza and you," I answered.

Her eyes blew up as I thought they would, as she processed my statement.

"Wha—what?" she gasped.

"You heard me," I said.

She collected her thoughts and suddenly became calm as if she was not surprised by my statement at all.

"Good. Your mom is coming to get Jamaal and the pizza will be here in forty-five minutes," she said.

I looked at her as she smiled at me.

"What if I would have said I wanted a burger?" I asked.

"You would have gotten pizza still," she replied, walking into Jamaal's room.

I shook my head. I knew she had something up her sleeve. It slipped my mind completely to ask her about all the flowers, balloons and cards. As I became engulfed in reading the numerous cards from friends and family members, my mother walked into the room.

"Boy, it ain't shit wrong with you. Get up out that der bed," she shouted.

I looked up and smiled as I began to slide up into a sitting position.

"No, baby, don't move. I was just joking. How are you?" she asked.

"I'm okay, Ma. And you?" I asked.

"Don't you worry bout this here ole lady. I'm striding...towards the good heavens that is," she said, chuckling to herself.

"Well, don't break out into a run, you hear me, lady?" I teased.

"Well, yeah, I do. But I believe the last time I checked the dipometer, you were the child and your little man was in there, peeing on everyone. So, you don't tell me what to do, BOY!" she joked.

"Yeess, ma'am," I said.

Jamaal ran into the room and jumped on my mother's lap.

"Nana, I'm going wit you!" he said proudly.

"Well, I guess you are. Are you ready to go now?" she asked him.

"Yeah, let's go," he responded.

"Good. Well you two be good. I'll have Jamaal back tomorrow night," Momma said, leaving the room but not before kissing my forehead.

"You get better," she whispered to me.

"I will, don't worry 'bout that," I responded.

Maria followed Momma and Jamaal to the door. The pizza delivery man must have been at the door because in no time Maria entered the room with a large box of pizza in her hand.

"Your food and wife is here, Mr. Lee, just as you had requested," Maria teased.

"Well, the pizza can wait...I want my wife now," I said.

Maria placed the pizza on the night stand and climbed on the bed. She straddled my lap.

"Oh, no you need to come and get under these brand new sheets you bought," I said, inviting her to join me.

When she pulled back the covers she was shocked to see me completely nude.

"Oh my damn. Were you like that when your momma came here?" she asked.

"Gurl naw, so my momma can pull back the covers and faint? I ain't her little boy no more! I took my pants off when y'all walked to the door," I informed her.

"Ooh," she said, climbing under the covers and straddling my naked body. I slowly began removing her clothes.

"You feel so good," I whispered in her ear.

I slowly began to kiss and nibble her ear as she kissed my chest. I slowly flipped her over and preceded to head down south to taste her love. I took my time and loved, kissed, tucked and licked her slowly. I could tell she was enjoying the feeling because she grabbed my head and pushed me closer towards her mound. I nibbled and pulled on her clit until she couldn't take it anymore and for the first time she ejaculated on my face. She was so stunned from the pleasure that she didn't notice me jump back, grab the end of the comforter and wipe my face. She was stunned from the feeling and I was stunned from almost going blind with her juices all in my eyes! She forced me to rejoin her in the bed. I obliged and, for the first time in a while, she returned the favor. She pulled and slurped my manhood like it was a blow pop. She tickled and fondled my balls with her hands as if she tried to find my bubble gum center. With one too many pops of the neck and flicker of the shaft, I exploded all over, without giving her a chance to duck. I laid back in bliss. Damn, this type of revenge is so sweet. Revenge is a bitch when you're on the other end. Who would have thought that she and I would have had enough energy to complete what we started, but we did.

"I'll let you rest. Just lay back and enjoy yourself," Maria seductively said.

I followed her request and took a deep breath. As soon as I had exhaled, she had slid down on my rock hard manhood. Her love felt so good I almost came that instant, but a brother got to hold his own! I looked over at the pizza on the night stand and

.ed. And just like that, the urge of climaxing was gone and anger set in. I looked back at Maria as she worked my joy stick. Little did she know, if it had not have been for that pizza, her game would have been over! I smiled as she did her magic. She felt so good, but I had to make her think she was in charge.

"Oh baby, you feel so good. You gonna cum with me?" she asked.

I pretended as if I didn't hear her. I grabbed her hips and assisted in gliding her along my shaft.

"Oh baby. Please cum with me," she begged.

Bingo. That's what I was looking for. The beg! I loved that!

"Tell me you want me to cum," I demanded as I pushed deeper and harder into her.

"I—I—waann—ooohhhh," she said while climaxing all over me.

Her muscles clenched around my manhood. I exploded inside of her love. We both laid back on the bed, exhausted.

"Damn, you know a brother just got out the hospital and you trying to put me back in!" I teased.

She climbed up beside me, laid her head on my chest and kissed it.

"Don't worry, I'll take care of you," she said.

I was really beginning to think that Maria really did care about me. Before long I fell asleep, not even thinking about the pizza that was probably cold as ice by this time.

I can't believe Anthony and I just had a time like that. That is how I've been wanting to act all along. It only took for him to go to the hospital to realize. Now look at him knocked out. It serves his right. People know not to play with good pussy as soon as you come off your sick bed. Anthony must have been misinformed! Nonetheless, I love him like this. I have wanted him like this all along. I laid back on the bed and closed my eyes I heard a buzzing noise and instantly knew it was my cell phone. I lifted the pizza box and grabbed the phone. I looked at the number and saw that it was Devonna. I slid out of the bed and crept into the den.

"Hello?" I whispered.

"Hey, baby. What you doing?" she asked.

"Nothing. Chillin'," I lied.

"Why you whispering?" she questioned.

"Anthony's home from the hospital and he's asleep. I don't want to wake him," I replied.

"Oh, he home? Where's baby boy?" she asked.

"With Ant's mom," I replied.

"Good. I'm coming to get you," she said.

"I'm chilling. I don't feel like going out," I said.

"Not even to see me?" she asked.

"Look, don't be like that. He did just get back from the hospital," I said.

"Can I have just an hour. I'll let you get back to playing house," Devonna sarcastically said.

"Fine. One hour, boo. That's it," I demanded.

"Okay. Be ready in twenty minutes," she said, hanging up the phone.

I rushed to the bed room. Anthony was still asleep. I took a quick shower and threw on some clothes. I wrote Anthony a short letter telling him that I'd be back. I grabbed my purse and headed out of the door. Devonna was pulling up as I was locking the door. I hurried to the car.

"Hey baby. What's up?" she asked, leaning over to kiss me.

"Nothing. Why was it so urgent for me to see you?" I asked.

"Because I wanted to. Is that a crime or are you done with us?" she asked.

The conversation had begun so quickly I had not noticed that we had started driving.

"No...I mean I don't know. Where are we going anyway?" I asked.

"Nowhere in particular, just driving. I miss you. Why do I get the feeling that you don't want me...this...us anymore?"

Devonna asked with a sound in here voice that I've never heard before. It scared me a little.

"Why would you get that feeling?" I asked.

I started to shift in the chair and then I looked out the window at all the trees wondering why we were riding the back streets of town, especially being that darkness was beginning to fall.

"You fucked him, didn't you?" she harshly asked.

"What? Wh—why do you say that betta yet, why does it matter?" I asked.

"Never mind, you've answered my question. DAMN, Lisa, what the hell do you want! Do you know? Do you now what the FUCK you really want?" Devonna yelled.

I was becoming very scared. I did not now what to expect. I had never seen her like this.

"Why are you yelling at me? You getting mad at me for making love to my husband?" I said calmly.

"Yeah, because just last week, you hated him, crying on my shoulder talking about leaving. Now you making love to him! What kindda shit is that?" she yelled.

I stayed quiet contemplating my next move. It really seemed to me that this psycho bitch was losing her damn mind!

Chapter 16

I woke up and glanced at the clock.

"Damn seven-thirty," I said to myself.

I sat up on the bed but heard nothing. The house was quiet. Too quiet. I got up and walked through the house. Maria was not around. "I know I didn't dream that shit," I said.

I walked back to the bed room and looked at the pizza box on the night stand. I instantly became hungry. I walked over to the box and saw a piece of paper on top. It was a letter from Maria.

Hey Baby,
I stepped out to the store.
I'll only be gone about an
Hour. Eat your food and
Chill out. I'll see you
Soon!
Love Ri

P.S. Don't leave the house!
I want another round!!!!

I placed the letter on the bed, grabbed the pizza box and headed towards the kitchen to warm a few slices up. While the pizza was in the microwave, I decided to look out of the window to see what car Maria took. I pulled three blinds down so that I could see the parking lot.

"What the hell?" I said.

Both cars were in the parking lot. It didn't make sense. If she was going to the store and would be back in an hour, how did she get there? I grabbed the two slices of pizza out of the microwave and ate them as I walked to the bedroom to put some clothes on. I threw on a pair of sweats and a hoodie. I found my Tims under the bed and put them on. I grabbed my car keys and waked out the door. Once I got in the car I picked up my cell phone and called Maria's cell. The phone rang until her voice mail came on. I did not leave a message. I hung up and called again. This time the phone rang for a minute and then she answered.

"Hello?"

"Where are you?" I asked, pulling out of the parking lot.

"Hey baby, what you doing? Why you calling me from your cell?" she asked.

"Look, how you gonna leave me a note talking 'bout you going to the store and you didn't drive none of the cars?" I asked.

"Um, well, I—I Devonna came and got me. I'm out with her," she said, stuttering.

"Why didn't you just say you were going out then?" I asked.

"Because I was gonna be home in an hour," she responded.

"And now?" I asked.

"Well—"

"Tell that nigga you'll be home Damn, we not finished here!" Devonna interrupted in the background.

Out of nowhere the phone hung up.

"What the hell is going on?" I screamed.

I didn't know what to do. I just kept driving. I was confused as hell and I needed to calm down. I kept driving and thought that the ride would calm me down.

"I can't believe you!" Maria screamed at Devonna after she hung up on Anthony.

Devonna held the phone in her left hand away from Lisa's reach.

"Look. That nigga can wait. This my damn time. He don't want your ass. He just want to fuck you. He don't love you. He don't care about you. Why you worried about that nigga, anyway?" Devonna yelled.

Maria became very upset and sat up in the chair. She took a deep breath.

"He is still my husband. And you are scaring me. Take me home," Maria demanded.

Devonna felt as if Maria was playing her and did not understand why Maria couldn't see that Anthony didn't love her like she did. Devonna kept driving as if she did not hear Maria.

"Damn it, I know you hear me. Turn this GOT DAMN car around now!" Maria screamed.

"Who the hell you bucking on? You don't want me to go off. Don't do this. This is a small street, Maria. Where can I turn around? The other lane is for opposite traffic," Devonna said, trying to be as calm as possible.

Maria sat back feeling as if she had accomplished something, but what it was she didn't know. All she knew was that Devonna was acting like a totally different person! Devonna kept driving, but she passed two places where she could have turned around.

"Look. That's the second place you could have turned and you didn't. Where are you taking me?" she asked.

"I don't know. We need to talk and I'm not taking you back until we do that!" Devonna said.

"Damn lie. You taking me back now!" Maria said.

Maria felt a sudden rush come over her and she grabbed the stirring wheel as hard as hard as she could and pulled. The car began to turn uncontrollably. Devonna and Maria screamed as Devonna's car circled quickly. The car suddenly stopped when it smashed head on into another car. The two women's bodies jerked back and forth from the crash.

"Yes. I am calling from Suffolk Boulevard. There has been an accident. A blue car and a black car has collided head on," the man reported on his cell phone to the 911 dispatcher.

"Sir, who are you?" she asked.

"I am Thomas," he answered.

"Well, Thomas, where are the people in the cars. How many are there?" the dispatcher asked.

"It looks like two in the blue car and one in the black one. But no one is moving," Thomas informed the dispatcher.

"How far down Suffolk Boulevard are you?" the dispatcher questioned.

"I am slap dab in the middle of the boulevard. Are you sending someone?" he asked in a hurry.

"Yes, sir. Emergency vehicles are on the way as we speak," she said.

Suddenly Thomas looked up and saw the flashing lights.

"Okay. They here," he said.

"Are you okay, sir?" she asked.

"Yeah, but I'm not to sure about the other people in those cars. The EMS workers are cutting the blue car," Thomas said.

"Okay. I can hang up now. Thank you for doing such a good job Thomas. The emergency people over there will handle the situation from that end," the dispatcher said, hanging up the phone.

An officer walked up to Thomas and began asking him questions.

"How you doing sir? Did you call 911?" he asked.

"Yes," Thomas replied.

"Did you see what happened? What's your name?" he asked.

"No sir, I didn't see the actual accident. I am Thomas," Thomas said, extending his hand to the officer.

They shook hands and Thomas continued with his story.

"I was driving in the right hand lane when I came up on the accident. I was the only car on the street at the time I arrived. I mean, people drove up after I called 911 but they did not stop. I don't now how long the accident was here," Thomas told the officer.

"Well, I'm officer Torres, I'm gonna give you my card now before I forget," he said, handing Thomas the card.

The officer proceeded. "I'm gong to get a little bit more information from you and if you remember something when you get home, make sure you call me," Officer Torres said.

Thomas nodded in agreement and answered the officer's questions. During the questioning an EMS worker walked over to Officer Torres and whispered in his hear.

"We have identified the bodies. They all had IDs on them," the worker said.

"I'll be right over," Officer Torres said.

The officer completed his questions and told Thomas he could leave. He saw the workers placing white sheets over all three bodies.

"All fatalities, uh?" Torres asked.

"Yes sir, they all died on impact," the worker responded.

"Damn. What are the names so we can notify next of kin," Torres asked.

"Over in the blue car we have Devonna Sell, the driver, and on the passenger side was Maria Lee. But peep this, over in the black car we have an Anthony Lee. Same address on the driving licenses," the worker reported. Torres raised his eyebrow, took the information and headed back to the station. While the scene was being cleared, Devonna, Maria and Anthony's bodies were taken to the morgue.

Torres arrived to the station and immediately began to search for the next of kin to notify. First he telephoned Devonna's mother, followed by Anthony's mother. The last person he had to call was Maria's parents.

"Hello, Mr. or Mrs. Fields, please," Torres asked.

"This is Mrs. Fields, how may I help you?" she asked.

"Ma'am, I am calling about your daughter and son-in-law," he said.

"Oh my GOD. He didn't kill her, did he?" she asked.

"No, ma'am—"

Mrs. Fields interrupted the officer. "She killed him?" she screamed.

"No, ma'am, let me finish. They were involved in a car accident. I'm sorry, ma'am, but they didn't survive the impact," the officer stated.

"Nooo. No. No. No. Where's the baby? Where's Jamaal?" Mrs. Fields screamed.

"Ma'am, it's to my understanding that he is with his paternal grandparents," Officer Torres informed her.

"Oh, my GOD. Oh my GOD. I can't believe this. Lord have mercy. Please have mercy on me!!!!" Maria's mother cried out.

"Ma'am I would need your and or Mr. Fields to go down to the morgue to identify the body of Mrs. Lee," he said.

"Okay. Where do I go?" she asked, attempting to calm down.

Officer Torres gave Mrs. Fields all the information she needed, apologized once more for her lost and ended the phone call. Mrs. Fields informed her husband of the despairing news. The two knelt down that instant and prayed. They collected their thoughts and emotions and traveled to the hospital to identify the body of their one and only child whom had left the earth so quickly and a child motherless.

Chapter 17

Word traveled pretty quickly about the accident. Within a day everyone knew about Anthony and Maria. Of course, Kim found out before Lisa and it took everything in her to tell Lisa the news the best she could. Kim drove to Lisa's apartment and knocked on the door. Lisa opened the door, dressed for church.

"Oh my GOD. You coming with me to church?" she said, leaving Kim at the door and walking to the bathroom to finish her hair. Lisa had not noticed the look on Kim's face. Kim took a deep sigh and walked into the apartment closing the door behind her.

"So what made you decide to go to church this morning?" Lisa yelled from the bathroom.

Kim sat down in the couch before she responded.

"Um, I'm not going to church Lis," Kim said slowly.

"What's wrong with you? Why you talking so slow? Things not working out with Shawn?" Lisa asked, continuing to perfect her hair.

"No, Shawn's cool. I think you need to come in here," Kim said.

"What is wrong with you?" Lisa huffed, walking into the den.

"You need to sit," Kim said quietly.

"For what? Kim, you are scaring me. What is wrong?" Lisa asked.

Lisa sat down beside Kim. Kim grabbed her hand and began rubbing it instantly between her own. Lisa immediately began to cry. She knew something was seriously wrong. Kim is only quiet when something is wrong.

"Don't cry, sis," Kim said with a tear in her eye.

"Just tell me, Kim, tell me," Lisa demanded.

Kim took a deep breath as tears began to flow from her solemn eyes.

"Lisa. There was an accident last night and Anthony was killed," Kim said.

There was total silence between the two women. Lisa stood up and shook her head. Kim silently sat there and watched.

"No. He's in the hospital, Kim. I talked to him before we went out the other night," Lisa said calmly.

"He came home, Lis, and the accident happened the same day he came home," Kim stated.

"What happened? Who did it? Are they in jail?" Lisa asked.

"Well, David told me that Anthony's wife left the house. He woke up and went looking for her. She was with her girlfriend and the police thinks that they were arguing in the car and some how lost control of it and it was the same time Ant was on the road and they hit head on. Everybody passed," Kim informed Lisa.

"It can't be—"

Before Lisa could complete her sentence she fell out on the floor crying. Kim got down on the floor with Lisa and turned her on her stomach, placing Lisa's head on her lap. Kim rubbed Lisa back for an hour as she cried. Lisa's telephone ran. Luckily the cordless phone was on the couch. Kim reached up and answered it.

"Hello?" Kim answered.

"Hey, K. I just wanted to make sure somebody was there with Lisa," David said softly.

"Yeah, I'm here. You okay?" Kim asked.

"Naw, but I'm trying to be strong," David replied.

"If you need me, call okay?" Kim said.

"Yeah. I'll be calling to tell you the arrangements," David said.

"Okay. I'll be here today and probably for a good while," Kim said.

"Tell Lisa to hang on, he's in a better place," David said forcibly.

"I will," Kim said.

Kim hung up the phone and looked down at Lisa. She had fallen asleep. Kim grabbed a pillow from the couch and placed it under Lisa's head. The phone rung again. Kim quickly answered the phone before it disturbed Lisa.

"Hello?"

"Kim, where Lisa at?" Rodney asked.

"Sleep," Kim said.

"Wake her up!" he said.

"For what?" Kim asked.

"She heard about Anthony and his wife and her girlfriend?" Rodney asked.

"Yeah and she sleep. And I'm not gonna wake her up!" Kim said.

"Well, let me ask you this, did she cry?" he asked.

"Yeah, of course why does it matter?" Kim asked.

"Should have known that," Rodney said.

"Look this is not the time to be jealous. Your fiancé is in pain and hurting, from the loss of a dear friend. You should be there for her," Kim said angrily.

"So I should come and baby her for crying ova anotha nigga?" Rodney said.

"You know what? Do what you want, I'm tired of trying to help someone who don't want to be helped! It doesn't matter who he is. All that matter is that was her friend and trust, you know just as well as I do that she'd be there for you!" Kim said before hanging up on Rodney.

"I can't believe that trifling dude," Kim said to herself.

She looked down at Lisa and she was still asleep. She began to look around the apartment for something to do. She couldn't clean because for the most part, Lisa kept the house clean. Kim laid on the couch to think about everything that was going on. As soon as she closed her eyes, her cell phone rang.

"Hello?"

"Hey cutie, y'all okay?" Shawn asked.

"Yeah, I'm good, Lisa sleep. How'd you now I was with her?" she asked.

"Because you have a good heart and I know you wouldn't leave your sister out," Shawn said.

"If you need something, just let me know," Shawn said.

"How'd you find out?" Kim asked.

"Well, the grapevine is rolling." Shawn chuckled.

"I bet. That's how black folks are," Kim said.

"Yeah, I know," Shawn said.

"Like I said if you need me call," he continued.

"I will. I will call you later," Kim said.

Lisa began to wake. She sat up and looked around.

"I got a banging headache," she said.

"Yeah, I understand. It's from all that crying," Kim said.

"Oh my GOD, so he's really gone?" Lisa asked.

She sat up against the couch.

"Yes, baby, he's gone," Kim replied.

Lisa laid her head on Kim's legs and sobbed.

"It's gonna be alright," Kim said.

"No, it won't. You don't understand. My heart is broken. A piece of me is gone forever. Kim, Anthony has always been a part of me. What am I going to do?" Lisa cried.

"Lisa, I know you love Anthony, but you have to move on. You have a fiancé. You can't dwell so much on the past. That trashes your future," Kim said, rubbing Lisa's head.

"Do you know where everyone is gathering?" Lisa asked.

"No, but I'll call David if you want me to," Kim said.

"No, I'll call," Lisa said, grabbing the phone.

Lisa dialed David's number still shaking from the shock of the news.

"What's up, baby girl?" David asked.

"I can't believe it, Dave. Why? Why does my heart have to be broken?" Lisa asked.

"Don't worry, Lisa. It'll mend and you best believe that Ant went out loving you like he's always told you he would," David said.

"Yeah, I know. Where y'all meeting?" Lisa asked.

"Well, being that my aunt and uncle really didn't care much for Ri and all, they will meet at their house, Ri's family will meet at Anthony and Ri's house, the services will be conjoined and they will be buried next to one another at Mae Whitley Memorial," David informed.

"Oh, okay. I'll probably go over to his peoples home tomorrow or so. It's Sunday, so I'm guessing the services will be Wednesday or Thursday?" Lisa stated.

"Um, naw, it's gonna be Tuesday," David said.

"What? That's soon," Lisa exclaimed.

"Yeah, I know, but Aunt Alice does not play and she don't believe in waiting forever to lay your loved one to rest," David replied.

Lisa took a deep sigh to regroup.

"Okay. So I'm guessing you know the place and time, too, uh?" Lisa asked.

"Yeah, Aunt Alice did that today. It will be at our church, United Christian Baptist at one o'clock," David said.

"Okay. I'm gonna chill out and collect my thoughts. I'll call you later," Lisa said.

"Okay. If you need me, call me," David said.

"I will, later," Lisa said.

"Peace," David returned.

Lisa put down the phone and looked at Kim.

"Everything is moving so fast," she said.

"I know. It's okay though. Don't worry," Kim replied.

Lisa got up and walked to her room. Kim remained in the den and turned on the television. Lisa stayed in the room for a while, but Kim did not move, she felt that Lisa needed time alone. Kim was preparing to relax on the couch when Lisa reappeared into the den with sweats and sneaker on.

"You going some where?" Kim asked.

"Yeah come take a ride with me," Lisa said.

Lisa grabbed her keys from on top of the television. Kim got up and followed Lisa out the door. The two women got into the car and Lisa began driving. The ride was very quiet with only Lisa's Musiq's Super Star CD playing softly in the back ground. After a short while, Lisa pulled into a school parking lot. She drove to the play ground, parked the car and got out. She stood in front of a rainbow shaped monkey bars. Kim joined Lisa after observing her blank stare.

"What in the world re we doing here at the elementary school?" Kim asked.

Lisa turned to face Kim. She had tears in her eyes.

"When I was younger, this used to be an intermediate school where fourth to six graders went. And this is where we met. Right here at these Monkey bars. We would also meet here to hug and kiss before and after school. See this little road?" Lisa asked, pointing at the small road they were standing on.

"Yeah," Kim said, looking to see where the road led.

Kim noticed that the road was a large circle that entered the school ground and also exited the school ground.

"This was the bus ramp. And our buses were always on this side of the ramp. That's why we met here," Lisa said.

She turned back around and slowly walked along the road. She lightly laughed.

"What's so funny?" Kim asked.

"I remember the both of us getting in trouble a lot because we were suppose to leave school and go straight to the buses or vice versa. No pit stops. But of course sometimes he got here before me or me before him. So we'd get fussed at from teachers for waiting around," Lisa said.

Lisa walked over to the monkey bars and sat on them. She took a deep breath and looked into the sky.

"I remember our first argument. He had given me a necklace with a charm on it. I don't even remember why I got mad at him." She laughed and continued.

"Anyway, I took the necklace off and got on the bus. When he got here to wait for me, I leaned my head out the window and threw it at him and told him I didn't want his mess," Lisa said, smiling.

She chuckled for a moment and looked at Kim.

"Girl, don't you know I had that damn necklace back around my neck the next week!" she said.

Kim walked over to Lisa and sat beside her.

"Lis, you know I'll always be here for you. And I'll always love you," Kim said.

"I know. That's what he told me, too," Lisa said.

She took a deep breath and slowly exhaled. She looked up into the sky.

"Do you still love me?" she said aloud.

Suddenly rain drops began to fall upon her face.

"I guess you got your answer, Lisa," Kim grunted before she got up and ran to the car.

Lisa stayed in the rain.

"This is how you tell me yes? Why couldn't you have a placed a pretty butterfly on my nose or something?" she asked out loud.

The rain stopped as sudden as it started and the wind began to lightly blow. Lisa smiled and walked to the car.

"Why'd you leave? You ain't sugar you wouldn't have melted," Lisa said to Kim as she got into the car and turned on the ignition.

"Ump. You don't know. Shawn would beg to differ," Kim teased.

"Thank you for coming with me. I needed to know. Especially before the service. I know this double service will be one for the books. Especially with her people. There will be whispers for day!" Lisa teased as they went back to Lisa's apartment.

"Yeah, but you don't worry about that you know what you and Anthony had and you know what y'all still have. He'll always love you," Kim insisted.

"I know," Lisa agreed, pulling up to her apartment.

Walking up to the door, Lisa looked at the ground, as she normally does, when she unlocked the door. But this day something was different. There was a single rose petal on the ground. Lisa bent down and picked it up. She rubbed the petal between her fore finger and thumb. She inhaled the sweet smell.

"What are you doing!?" Kim asked.

Lisa opened the door, walked in and went straight to the kitchen.

"I found this on the doorstep," Lisa said, showing Kim the petal.

"You don't have no rose trees over here," Kim said.

"I know. I know my baby sent it," Lisa said.

"Rodney? He's so cheap! Where's the rest of the roses?" Kim teased.

"No! Anthony. How would one rose petal get over here?" Lisa said.

Lisa took out some lamination paper to preserve the petal.

"Only you would have lamination paper in the house!" Kim teased.

"You never know. The dollar store sell it. why not have some on hand?" Lisa responded.

Kim laughed and shook her head.

"Girl, you crazy," Kim said.

Lisa walked into the den with the laminated flower petal and sat on the couch holding the petal.

"Damn, I can't believe he's gone K," Lisa said sadly.

"I know, but you'll see him again," Kim said.

The two women sat back on the couch glaring at the television in silence.

Chapter 18

Tuesday arrived a lot quicker than Lisa hoped. She was taking her time to prepare.

"Lisa, you okay? We're leaving in ten minutes," Kim yelled from the den.

"Okay. I'm ready now," Lisa said, entering the den from the bathroom.

Kim was stunned at how beautiful Lisa looked. She smiled.

"Do I look okay?" Lisa asked.

"Girl, you trying to make people hot with you for real! You look real good," Kim said.

A knock on the door interrupted their conversation. Lisa walked to the door and opened it.

"Damn, girl. You go! You gonna let that man know what he missing on earth!" Lynelle screamed.

"Girl, you silly!" Kim said, getting up to join Lisa and Lynelle.

"Y'all ready?" Lynelle asked.

"Yeah," Kim and Lisa replied in unison.

The three women walked to the car in silence. The ride to the church was the same. Once Lynelle reached the parking lot of the church, Lisa immediately began to feel sick.

"Y'all. I can't do this, y'all. My stomach hurts," Lisa said.

"Look, girl, you are strong, black, and beautiful. You can get through this. You can do this. We are her for you," Lynelle said, parking.

"Yeah, you can do this," Kim agreed.

Lisa got out of the car and walked around to the front of the church. Kim and Lynelle closely followed. Lisa went to walk into the church to have a sit, when she was stopped by Mr. and Mrs. Lee and David.

"Lisa, come here, girl," Mr. Lee said.

Lisa walked over to Anthony's father. Kim and Lynelle waited on the side.

"Hi, Mr. and Mrs. Lee. I am sorry about things. I will truly miss him dearly," Lisa said.

"For what, baby? You didn't do it. Anthony always had good things to say about you!" Mrs. Lee stated.

Mr. Lee leaned over and whispered in Lisa's ear.

"I've always told that boy he should have married you," he said.

"Look, you need to be over in this line with us. You are family and will always be. Ain't that right double A?" David said to Anthony's mother.

"You right. Lisa get your friends and y'all get in this line, get right over there with David and Daniel," Mrs. Lee demanded.

Lisa, Kim, and Lynelle followed Mrs. Lee's directions. The line began to precede into the church. First to walk in was Anthony's parents, followed by David, Lisa, Lynelle, Kim, Daniel, and rest of Anthony's family. Maria's family had entered the church earlier and were already seated. As soon as Lisa entered the church the whispering began. Lisa began to breath heavy. Dave grabbed her hand.

"Don't worry. You got haters everywhere," David said.

Lynelle rubbed Lisa's back to let her know the support was there. They all had a seat and for the first time Lisa was seeing Anthony since she had seen him in the hospital. David and Lynelle both leaned over at the same time and asked Lisa if she was okay. She nodded her head in the affirmative. Lisa leaned over to David.

"Where's Rita?" she asked.

"She don't do funerals so she's at Aunt Alice and Uncle James's house with the kids and family who couldn't bare coming," he replied.

"Oh. He looks asleep," she said.

"Yeah, he does," David replied.

The pastor stood and shared his meaning on death and how we will see our love ones again. He then gave representatives from both families time to highlight Anthony and Maria's lives. Maria's cousin was the first to speak.

"I would like to start off saying that Maria was a very lovely woman. She always cared about other's feelings and emotions. She was a wonderful mom and a terrific wife."

"Umph, who she think she fooling?" one of Anthony's female cousins said under her breath.

Maria's cousin paused and then continued.

"Maria gave life when those weren't willing to do so," she paused again and looked directly in to Lisa's eyes. Lisa looked down in her lap.

"No that heffa didn't," Lynelle said under her breath.

"It's okay, Nell, just smile," Lisa said, following her own advice looking back up at Maria's cousin.

Maria's cousin proceeded with her speech.

"Lastly, she was loved by most but respected by all. I can honestly say that she will be dearly missed, but I don't feel she would have wanted to go with anyone but who she went with…her loving husband," she completed.

"Oh and all this time, I thought she died in a crash with her lesbian lover!" Kim said under her breath.

"Amen. A-Man!" Lynelle and Daniel said loudly above every one.

Maria's cousin sat down and David got up.

"Oh, Lord. David, don't act ugly," Kim said to David.

"I won't!" David said.

David reached the mic and behaved like only David could.

"Amen saints," David said.

"Amen," the congregation softly responded in unison.

"I don't think y'all heard me. I said A-MEN, Saints!" David repeated louder.

"Amen," the congregation stated louder.

"What can I say about my best friend, cousin, my brother? Let me first say that Anthony is a good man. I'm saying is because now he's in the room upstairs helping the big man with working on the rest of us down here. Anthony worked hard at everything he did. Not only did her work hard, he loves hard. If Anthony has ever told you he loved you, he meant it. And you best believe it is forever. Anthony never used the word lightly. He had different levels of love. There are some people he'll love forever even beyond the end of time." David paused and looked at Anthony's parents and Lisa.

"And there are some that he loves because he believes in the love of family and dear friends. Lastly, there are those he loves to like." David paused once again and looked at Maria's family.

"Lastly, I would like to say that everyone here has been impacted by the love of Anthony, whether it was directly or indirectly and if we did not love him...or Maria for that matter...we would not be here. Thank you," David said.

David slowly walked to his seat. Lisa patted him on his knee and whispered to him.

"You did a good job!" Lisa told him.

"Thanks. I just spoke the truth," he whispered back.

One of Lisa and Anthony's school mates, Kesha, sang "His Eye Is on the Sparrow", which brought tears to everyone's eyes. Lastly, it was time to view the bodies. The ushers stood beside the pew that David, Daniel and the girls were sitting on, indicating that it was their time to view the body before exiting the church. David grabbed Lisa by one hand and Lynelle grabbed the other and walked her to Anthony's casket. The casket was a beautiful navy blue with snow white interior. Anthony was dressed in an all white suite with a silk blue shirt and silk blue handkerchief, folded neatly in the upper left hand side of the suite. Lisa stared endlessly at him. She believed he was so beautiful laying there peacefully. He did not look dark or disfigured like people often do at funerals. He looked just like the Anthony she remembered years ago, when they first met. Beautiful brown skin and almost perfect bone structure. Lisa could not take the image any longer. She blinked and immediately broke down. He knew buckled from under her. David caught her before she hit the floor.

"Hoooold up. I got you," he said, firmly holding her.

"Come on, baby girl, let's get it together," Lynelle whispered in Lisa's ear while helping David escort her away from the casket and out the door of the church. Once Lisa was outside of the church door she took a whiff of fresh air and felt slightly better.

"Okay. You straight, Lisa?" David asked.

"Yeah," she responded.

"We'll just follow y'all to the burial grounds," Lynelle said to David.

"Aight," David said.

David turned around just in time to see Daniel and Kim exiting the church. Kim's eyes were swollen and Daniel was rubbing back.

"I'm okay. Thanks, Danny," Kim said.

Kim caught up with Lisa and Lynelle and the women walked to Lynelle's car to prepare to travel to the burial grounds. When the women arrived to Lynelle's car, Rodney was leaning on the back of his car with his legs crossed and arms folded across his chest.

"Look who's here!" Lynelle said.

Lisa blinked from amazement. She could not believe Rodney was there. Kim walked passed Rodney, without speaking, and got in the car. Lynelle looked at Lisa and whispered in her ear, "You gonna be okay?"

"Lisa nodded her head. Lynelle looked at Rodney and back at Lisa.

"Don't be too long, don't forget we're following Dave and Danny," she said loud enough for Rodney to hear her.

Lynelle got in the car leaving Rodney and Lisa alone.

"You okay?" Rodney asked.

"I will be," Lisa responded

"Look, I'm sorry about the last couple of days, and I know this isn't the right time to discuss me, you and our problems—"

"Your problems," Lisa interrupted.

"Okay, my problems, Anyway, we do need to talk, just not now. I wanted to let you know I'm here for you if you want me to come over later on," Rodney said.

Rodney took his hand and lifted Lisa's head so that they could see eye to eye. He looked her straight into her eyes.

"I love you," he said.

Lisa did not respond. Rodney's hand continued to prop her face.

"Don't think anything less. You don't have to say it in return. Just know that I do. Okay?" Rodney said.

Rodney gently kissed her lips and whispered in her ear, "Call me."

Lisa nodded and Rodney walked off. Lisa entered the car to complete silence. Just as Lynelle began to ask her first question, David pulled up beside her and blew his horn.

"Well, ladies, let's go," Lynelle said.

The drive to the cemetery was short because it was about two blocks from the church. When the girls exited the car David and Daniel were waiting. They all walked to the tent together. Mrs. Lee patted the seat next to her and looked at Lisa. Lisa looked around and behind her. David looked back at her and whispered.

"You've always been family."

Lisa took a deep breath and looked at Daniel. He nodded and she took the seat. Anthony's mother leaned over to Lisa and patted her knee.

"Don't worry, sweetheart, he'll always be looking on you," his mother said.

Lisa thought to herself for a moment and then wondered if he would become upset when she was with someone else sexually and throw things at her. The thought made her smile. She turned to Mrs. Lee and looked her in her eyes.

"I know!" she said smiling.

The pastor began the common burial speech. All Lisa heard was, "Blah, blah, blah. Blah, Blah," as she gazed at the casket that concealed her very first love. Lisa did hear the end of the speech that everyone knew so well because everyone mouthed it with the pastor.

"Ashes to ashes, dust to dust," the pastor quoted boldly.

When the pastor concluded the ceremony and ordered everyone to return to their vehicles, Lisa remained seated. She could not move. Anthony's parents stood up. Mr. Lee, walked over and hugged Lisa. Mrs. Lee, holding the US flag that the soldiers folded from the top of Anthony's casket, leaned over and kissed Lisa on the cheek.

"You are always welcomed in our home baby....always' she said before leaving.

Lisa remained seated. David looked at her sadly.

"You ready to go," he asked.

"I want to see them lower him," she said softly.

"Okay," David said, walking away to inform Lynelle and Kim of Lisa's request. Lynelle, Kim, David, and Daniel stepped back and allowed Lisa to watch the ground keepers lower Anthony's casket into the ground.

"My love so sweet and true. My love, there will be no one quite like you. My love so dear, who would have thought? That up in Heaven you would be caught, to be with GOD I know you'll be...so sleep my love...sleep peacefully," Lisa recited until she could no longer see the casket from her seat. Lisa stood up with tears falling continually from her eyes. She turned around with the look of helplessness in her eyes. The whole group walked over to her and gave her a huge group hug.

"Enough of all this sad shit...let's get some drinks," David yelled.

"I second that emotion," Lynelle said.

"I know you do!" Kim replied.

"What you gonna do, chick?" Lynelle asked Lisa.

"Let's go," Lisa responded.

The group all headed to their cars on the way to Tony's to celebrate the love and life of their special friend, family member and in some case...brother.

RIP.... Anthony Lee
After the Love Is Gone

Much to Lisa's surprise, her life had changed drastically. She thought that after the services, she'd be unable to move on with her life and her life would not be as difficult because she did not have Anthony popping in and out of her life. She had one month before her sophomore year at a brand new school. Although the school is local and she's familiar with the area, she knew that she would have to be focused because she had all her friends to get her off track.

Every now and then Lisa thought about Anthony. She thought about if she knew the real story behind the car crash. Kim was told by David all that he was told, which was Anthony went home from the hospital, made love to Maria. Maria left to be with her lover, which happened to be a woman, the two argued and ended up crashing into Anthony, who was riding to find Maria. Lisa thought the story was odd. She still couldn't believe that her first love was gone. She visited Anthony's grave regularly, always praying that she could make it through. Some how Anthony's and Maria's parents worked it out to have joint custody of Jamaal. Whenever she got a chance, Lisa visited him at the Lee's home. She wasn't sure if Anthony's parents tried to explain to their grandson who she was but loved to visit him and hear his energetic voice yell…"Hey, Auntie Lisa."

It almost bought tears to her eyes when ever she would leave him. Some times when she got home she would wonder what Anthony and Maria, especially Maria, thought about her interacting with Jamaal. Although, it was scary to Lisa at times, she felt a certain calmness with Jamaal that she did not have around anyone else.

Lisa walked into her apartment from working eighteen hours at the department store. She closed the door and looked down on the floor. She was stepping on a envelop. She bent down to pick it up. It read…*To Auntie Lisa* on the front. Lisa curiously opened it. It was a pretty pink card with white clouds and sparkles of rain falling on a bare ground. The words on the front of the card read, *Let the Lord's sparkling teardrops absorb into your soul…* Lisa smiled and opened the card. The inside had a picture of hearts on tall stems with smiley faces on them. The card continued from the front. *And make your heart smile with thoughts that someone loves you!* And it was signed… *Love, Jamaal,* at the bottom. Lisa took the card and placed it on top of the television with one single tear in her left eye. She smiled, laid on the couch and closed her eyes to sleep. Right before she dozed off, she whispered, "I love you, too, baby," knowing that the statement was for both Jamaal and Anthony.

Rules

188 608

23 99